THE SKY OVER CHAOS

Short Stories by Markus McDowell

Markus McDowell

An Imprint of Sulis International Press

Los Angeles | London

THE SKY OVER CHAOS:
SHORT STORIES BY MARKUS MCDOWELL
Copyright ©2019 by Markus McDowell. All rights reserved.

Cover design by Sulis International
Artwork by Linda Zupancic

Library of Congress Control Number: 2019903035
ISBN (paperback): 978-1-946849-40-3
ISBN (eBook): 978-1-946849-41-0

Riversong Books
An Imprint of Sulis International
Los Angeles | London

www.sulisinternational.com

If you are interested in other writings by
Markus McDowell
join his mailing list at
https://markusmcdowell.com/newsletter-2/

Novels by Markus McDowell

To and Fro Upon the Earth: A Novel

Onesimus: A Novel of Christianity in the Roman Empire

Contents

THREE DAYS

"Oh, no. Not Clementine."

He dropped his head and sobbed. The letter fluttered from his hand to the floor, falling open. The words of the page stared up at him.

A mere two days after you left, my dearest John. The Diphtheria took her swiftly. I left the others with Beth and went into town in the snow. No doctor available until next month. Paterson told me to mix a concoction of garlic juice and salt, which I did, but to no wise purpose. Our sweet daughter is gone. With no priest at the church, and you away, it took me three days to build a little casket and dig the cold grave. Please come soon. I fear for the other three.

Your loving wife, Becky

•••

She remembered that some boards were left over from the shed John built three years ago. A quick search located the stack inside the shed itself. In the back, covered by a tarp with a few items to hold it down. She moved them: a hammer, a piece of iron chain, a bag of seeds, and a small glass bottle with a glass stopper. She unstopped it. Sweet smell, but strong enough to make her eyes water. The white label read "trichloromethane" in John's handwriting.

With John's saw, she cut four long pieces and two short ones. A length of spinning yarn made a good measure for making sure each set matched in size. She knew how to brace the pieces and nail them together from having helped John build the shed. Still, it was slow work. She did not have the strength or experience of her husband.

At noon, she went to the ranch house and made lunch for the girls. The four of them ate in silence at the kitchen table, keenly aware of the empty place and the body in the next room. No one spoke. Gertrude sniffled.

I cannot do this, Becky thought. *He should never have left in winter. I cannot protect four girls.* She slammed her hand on the table, and the three girls jumped. Three sets of eyes, afraid.

A pain in her heart brought her up. "Oh, my dears. I'm sorry. I am just tired. You keep eating, I'm going back to work. Beth, watch them, please." She could always depend on Beth as the oldest, though she was only seven.

She finished the small casket around sundown, though it was hard to tell the time because of the thick clouds. Leaving the box in the shed, she trudged back to the house. The thick crust of snow crunched like peanuts under her feet.

Little Gertrude and Miriam were fast asleep. She said goodnight to Beth and fell into her bed.

•••

Digging the frozen earth was more difficult than building a small casket. Far more difficult. She knew that six feet of depth was required, though she didn't know why. Every two hours she dropped the shovel and slogged to the house to pull off her gloves and sit by the fire. Once her bones warmed up, she went back out.

At the end of the first day, she was halfway done. Beth met her at the door.

"Miriam's coughing bad, mama."

A vise gripped her heart as she ran upstairs. The girl was tucked into bed with a blanket to her neck.

"Miriam, my love, do you have a sore throat?"

She nodded. Her little brown curls were plastered against her forehead. Becky peered inside her mouth. No gray-white patches. Yet.

I can't watch this again. The waiting is excruciating. It will kill me.

Beth came in with a cold cloth, and Becky placed it on the little girl's head.

"Thank you, Beth. Please bring me the bottle beside Clementine's bed." She paused. "It's garlic juice."

"Momma?" Gertrude, from the bed across the room.

"Yes, dear?"

"Is Miriam going to die, too?"

•••

The train belched and grew quiet—an ominous silence. John made his way down the aisle and onto the platform. Even under the awning, the snow had piled up , though someone had made an effort to remove it.

He clumped into the station house and to the front desk.

"Greetings, Emily. Do you know if anyone is headed out towards my place?"

"I doubt you'll find anyone, John. It's bad out there."

He nodded and left the station, making for the General Store. It was just after noon, and the windows were shuttered. Paterson never missed a meal.

Pulling his cloak tighter around him, he walked over to the hotel, kicking his way through the snow. The lobby was full of people drinking tea and whiskey warmed by a blazing fire. A warm oasis from the fury of nature.

"John, thought you were in the capitol?" That was William, the owner and clerk.

"I received a letter from Becky that we lost one of our girls to diphtheria."

"Sorry to hear that." William shook his head. "It's such a ravage. James and Bonnie lost their son last winter, if you remember. I heard that Queen Victoria lost two grandchildren just last year to it."

"I need to get out to my place. You know anyone going that way?"

"No one's going out. The ford is frozen over and no one'll risk their horses. No reason to go out if you don't have to."

"I have to. Guess I'll walk it."

"I'll get you a skin of hot tea and whiskey to take. It'll be a cold four miles."

•••

Her hands shook, making it hard to read from the prayer book. Beth and Gertrude stood across the grave. She had made Miriam stay in bed.

"Unto Almighty God," she read, "we commend the soul of our sister departed, and we commit her body to the ground; earth to earth, ashes to ashes, dust to dust..." She faltered as Beth coughed, glancing up and back down. It was not the correct prayer for a child. But she couldn't find it.

I can't do this. I can't endure the waiting.

Three days to build a coffin and dig a grave. Three days of work in the chill snow.

"...in sure and certain hope of the Resurrection unto eternal life, through our Lord Jesus Christ, at whose coming in glorious majesty to judge the world, the earth and the sea shall give up their dead and the corruptible bodies—"

Gertrude began to cry. *How could God ask a mother to watch her children suffer and die a slow death of suffocation?*

"...and of those who sleep in him shall be changed, and made like unto his own glorious body—"

•••

She found that cutting twelve long pieces and eight short ones one after the other was easier than doing four and two at a time. Her piece of yarn had become dirty and ragged from measuring.

Digging, too, seemed easier if she alternated between the different spots. It didn't lessen the volume of dirt to move, but it made her feel better. When she wasn't digging, she laid the large tarp over the site to warm the earth underneath and make digging easier.

She worked all day, every day. By the light of a lantern, she could work in the shed before dawn and after dusk. Beth complained, but Becky told her to stay in bed, despite her protests that she did not have a sore throat and felt fine. She even offered to help her mother. Becky would not hear of it.

She had to do it alone. It was her duty. To prepare them. From a corruptible sleep to a glorious body.

Beth would understand. Eventually.

•••

His hands were numb as he crossed the little creek at the edge of their property. He'd drunk the last of the tea and whiskey at the ford. William had been right—it was frozen. Thick in some places and thin in others.

He cut a sturdy, straight branch from a nearby tree and used it to test the surface as he made his way across. Once, he panicked when the ice cracked beneath his feet. It couldn't be more than three feet deep, but wet trousers in the cold and snow was a recipe for pneumonia. He backtracked and found another way across thicker ice.

Another ten minutes and he spotted the farmhouse. Threads of smoke from the chimney swirled in the angry wind.

As he drew close, the door to the shed opened, and a figure backed out, pulling something heavy. A wooden box. He ran to her.

"Becky! Becky!"

She turned and stopped, a frozen figure in a frozen land. A cloud of snow erupted as she dropped the box. She ran to him in awkward leaps, legs splaying out and in through the fresh powder, calling his name. She called his name, her voice frail and small in the wind.

She was his arms, a bundle of furs and cloaks. "Oh, John. Three days it took! Three days to make a coffin and dig a grave. I couldn't watch."

Her breath was warm against his neck, coming in ragged sobs.

"It's okay, Beck. I'm here."

"No, it's not…three days while…three days…"

●●●

He helped her inside to sit in the big chair beside the fire. He went and shut the door, then stoked the fire. Becky stared at the floor, her mouth moving.

"Becky? What are you saying?"

She looked up, eyes wide like a trapped animal.

"All four John…all four…it took three days to build a coffin and dig a grave. Three days of waiting, John…"

He stepped back. "All four? Where…where are they?"

She pointed towards the west wall.

He took her shoulders, he leaned down. "Becky, look at me."

Her eyes were empty, as if she no longer saw him.

"Where?"

"By old Brownie."

"Where we buried old Brownie?"

She nodded.

He pulled his coat around him tight and went out.

•••

Four crude wooden crosses stuck into the ground. Skewed right and left. Four mounds of dirt. Four little girls. Four voids in life.

As he drew closer, he saw that the fourth grave was not filled in. The mound of dirt sat beside it, waiting. John stopped at its foot. Which girl had survived the longest? Where was her body? Surely not in the coffin Becky had been dragging.

He went back inside and found his wife as he'd left her.

"Becky?"

She didn't move.

"Becky, who was the last one? Where is she?"

Without looking up, she whispered. "Gertrude."

"Where is she?"

Someone coughed upstairs.

John took the stairs two at a time. Gertrude lay in her little bed, drooping eyes. "Daddy."

He ran to her and hugged her, "Oh, Gerty, my dear girl." He tried not to cry. She seemed—

"Open your mouth, dear." She obeyed. He examined her throat. No sign of discoloration or patches. "Gerty, do you have a sore throat?"

She closed her eyes and shook her head.

"Fever?"

No answer. He let out a sob and stood, stepping back to look down at a small glass bottle with a label on the floor.

TURN AND FACE THE CHANGE

He'd heard the story from his mom when she was still alive. After her husband died, she started collecting bugs. Every kind imaginable. The thing was, they were alive. And not in tanks or containers. Just loose. In her house. When no one had seen her for weeks, the neighbors broke in and found her dead, and the house crawling with bugs.

She'd left food out for them, though. And had made little beds out of cardboard and paper.

But Charlie wasn't collecting bugs.

•••

Charlie loved his house. He liked the way he had repainted the exterior every year, on the same weekend. Always the same colors—colors he had chosen with care so that they complemented each other in a way that pleased the eye. He liked that the hedges and grass were trimmed, watered, and fertilized on a regular schedule. It satisfying to see it all so well-put-together. Thought. Planning. Attention to detail.

He knew not everyone cared as much as he, and that was okay. "To each his own," he would say, when a neighbor would comment on how beautiful his house was compared to theirs. "Some people focus on their house, others focus on work, others on friends and family. We can't do everything. We make choices." That seemed to make them feel better.

But he didn't believe that. He applied that approach to everything. His car. His office. His exercise schedule three days a week for precisely one hour (as recommended by his doctor). Which television shows he watched, and for how long. The books he read for forty-five minutes each day (as suggested by a therapist he had once consulted about stress).

And it wasn't only physical things. There were specific procedures for work. How he dealt with problems. How he dealt with each task. It was the same in all aspects of his life.

It all mattered. Why *shouldn't* one pay attention? Have a sound process for everything. It made life so much easier.

So when he said, "To each his own," he was only being kind. Everything could be orderly. People were just lazy.

Cynthia said he was being judgmental. "Oh, Charlie, you just have a brain that works that way. Most people don't—it doesn't mean they are lazy or unintelligent!" She'd remind him that Einstein had a sloppy desk and was a genius who changed the field of mathematics.

But he didn't have *to have a sloppy desk*, Charlie thought. *He would have accomplished even more if he'd had a system.*

•••

"Charlie, don't forget we have that little get-together with the Phillips tonight. The new couple?"

He paused at the door, briefcase in hand. "Yes. It is on my calendar. I'd prefer to watch the game tonight—Brewers are in the playoffs, you know. But I can catch the end."

She smiled. "Good. See you tonight." She kissed him on the cheek.

He checked the mailbox before getting in his car. As he always did.

The box was empty.

He stood still, unsure of what to do. It was not possible there was no mail on a weekday. Even junk mail came every day.

"Good morning, Charlie!" Charlie turned. It was Jim, his neighbor across the street, walking to his car.

Charlie waved. "How are you today, Jim?"

"Quite well, thank you."

"Jim, my mailbox is empty. It's never empty. Did you get the mail today?"

"It doesn't come until the afternoons."

Charlie frowned. "No, it always comes in the morning."

Jim looked amused. "Well, mine doesn't. Afternoon. I always get it when I arrive home from work."

Charlie thought, *It comes in the morning, you just don't check it until after work.* But his wife's voice in his head said, "Don't be rude," so he just nodded. "Okay. Have a nice day, Jim."

On the way to work, Charlie pondered the possibilities. Perhaps they *didn't* get any mail today. An unusual confluence of events, perhaps. Maybe the post office had delayed today. Or the mail person had an accident.

He parked in his usual spot, entered through the big glass doors, and said hello to Barclay, the building receptionist, as he always did. Glancing at his watch, he saw he had made the trip from home two minutes faster today. He could spend a little more time in the coffee shop on the bottom floor, where he always ordered an Americano with a splash of cream.

Susan was behind the counter, as usual, though sometimes it was Mohammed, the owner. That day was Monday, but Charlie noticed that sometimes Mohammed was not there on Mondays, but on Tuesdays. Mohammed had been running the shop for four years (next month). His coffee was better than any other place Charlie had tried.

Susan handed him his coffee, he paid with exact change, as always, then took the third elevator (on the left) to the seventh floor.

Down the hall, fifth door on left, he opened the door with the sign that said, "Bower and Pottsdam, Forensic Accountants." Underneath were the names of the four partners, one of which was his: Charlie Chesterton. When he joined the firm, his goal was to make partner between four and five years later. It took four years and seven months and three days.

He pushed on through, greeted Kailee at the front desk, and strode back to his office (third door on the right, just after a soiled spot on the carpet which should have been replaced a year ago). He opened his office door and stopped.

Something wasn't right.

He scanned the room. His desk. The computer was in the center of the desk, not on the left. That was best for work ergonomics.

He moved behind the desk. His coffee cup, washed and dried at the end of the last workday, was on the left, not the right. A pad of paper was out—which he always put in the drawer before he left work.

Suspicious, he opened the drawers. Everything was as it should be (except the pad of paper.) He explored the rest of the office. Everything else was normal.

He headed back out to the reception room.

"Kailee, was someone using my desk?"

She looked up from her computer. "Not that I know of. Why?"

"Everything was moved around."

She frowned. "Everything?"

"Well, no." He cringed inside. He hated imprecise language. "Computer, coffee cup, a pad of paper."

"Oh. Well, I don't know. Maybe you just forgot—" she saw the expression on his face "—maybe ask Parson. I think he was here late last night."

Parson was in the break room. "Good morning, Parson."

Parson turned around from the coffee machine with a strange expression. No, not a strange expression. No expression.

"Good…morning." He cocked his head sideways, as if unsure of something.

"Do you know if anyone used my office? It's not a big deal, just that someone moved my things around."

"Your office? Which one is it?"

Charlie laughed. Parson did not. "Third one on the left as you come in. With my name on it."

Parson still looked confused. "No, not that I am aware. I was here late, but I was the only one after hours. And the doors were locked. Did you ask Kailee?"

"Yes."

"Ah, well. Nothing missing?"

"No."

"No harm. Maybe you just forgot." He turned back to the coffee pot.

Charlie stood for a moment, frowning. Was he hiding something? He didn't seem…himself. But if he'd used his office, why not just tell him? Nothing was missing, and there was no damage.

He went back to his office to restore his belongings to their rightful places and begin work.

•••

He thought about Parson as he drove home. Was he mad at Charlie for some reason? They had worked to-gether for many years. Even out to a bar for drinks after work a few times. Why would—

An angry horn sounded from behind. A green sedan showed in the rearview mirror, with a driver motioning at him to go. He looked up at the light. It hadn't changed—

There was no light. Where was the light? This was the four-way stop at Clover and Power Street. But there was no light. He hadn't looked, of course, just stopped out of habit. He glanced over at the street sign—was he confused as to where he was? No. It was Power Street.

The horn sounded again, longer this time. He checked for cross traffic and accelerated into the intersection. Why would the city remove a traffic light? They were always adding them—not subtracting. And this was a busy intersection.

•••

He wife came out of the kitchen as he arrived home.

"Hi! We need to be at the Freeman's in twenty minutes."

Charlie stopped. "You changed your hair!"

She made a face. "What? No, I didn't."

"Yes. The blonde or gray streaks. I like it."

She guffawed. "I haven't done anything different with my hair in years. But thanks for not noticing." She pretended to be insulted.

"Those gray streaks weren't there."

She put her hand on his chest. "Aw, how sweet of you not to notice. I'm still the young girl you married." She laughed. "Come on, we need to go."

He loved her luxurious brown hair. He played with it sometimes. He'd have noticed. Maybe she thought it was vain. Though she knew he did not mind when she spent money on beauty or other treatments.

•••

"That was nice, wasn't it?" his wife said, as they walked back from the Phillips home.

"Yes, it was. I've always liked Tory and Tony."

"Because their names are so melodious?"

He laughed. "Perhaps. But also because they are smart and not drama queens."

"Yes, they are fun to be around. When did they move here? Wasn't it right after we did?"

"Yes, just a few months after."

He opened the door for her. She went upstairs to change and said she'd be right down to watch the game with him—they were both Brewers fans. Charlie sat down and turned on the television. The game should be about halfway through. He searched the guide and found "MLB Division Series" and selected it. This was Phillies and Marlins playing. He was pretty sure the Phillies didn't even make the playoffs. Where was the Brewer's game? He searched the guide again, but it was the only baseball game on. Maybe he was wrong about the night? Maybe this was an old game being re-played—they did that sometimes. He called up the info on the television.

No. It was live. Phillies and the Marlins. In Philadelphia. Game Two,

He heard his wife behind him. "What's the score?"

"I—I don't know. This is Rockies-Marlins, not Brewers-Marlins. I don't think—didn't think the Rockies made the playoffs."

"Well, I wondered why you wanted to see the game. You were so mad last week when they lost the series and were out of the pennant run."

He looked up at her. She was looking at him without expression. She was not joking.

His heart was beating hard. Something was wrong. He didn't remember the Brewers losing a series last week. He didn't even—

"Charlie, are you okay?"

He looked up. "Yes. Yes. Just a long day. Guess I forgot."

She laughed and patted him on the head. "You are often forgetful when you are busy at work."

Work wasn't busy this week. And Charlie was never forgetful.

•••

He checked every intersection on the way to work for traffic lights, stop signs, even the street names. Checking his memory. Testing his mind.

He didn't *feel* like there was anything wrong with him.

So far, every street, light, and landmark was just as he remembered. He relaxed. Maybe it was a fluke. A glitch in his brain. Or the result of overwork or not much sleep.

He pulled up to the last stop sign before turning onto the street where the office sat. A stop sign. Just as it should—

The street's name was different "Elmendorf." That wasn't right. It was Pemerton. It had always been Pemerton. He glanced around, thinking maybe he'd passed the street and was at the further intersection. But, no. There was the old red-brick medical building on the far corner. The Mobil gas station on the opposite corner.

Heart pounding, he turned onto the street and saw his office building ahead. He took a deep breath. Maybe they had changed its name. and he had never noticed . He wasn't sure why, but sometimes cities *did* change street names. It was probably no big deal. Right?

Inside, Kailee frowned when he asked her about the street. "It's been the same ever since I've been here. Look on your business card."

He hadn't considered that. He pulled one out of his wallet.

Charlie Chesterton, Certified Public Accountant
Partner, Bower and Pottsdam, Ltd
4589 Elmendorf, Suite 705
Raleigh, NC 27545

"Charlie? Are you okay?"

•••

He sat at his desk, staring at the wall. It was almost noon. Maybe he had a stroke and didn't know it. That happened, right? Could it affect his memory? He wasn't sure.

He should call his doctor and have him run tests. He picked up the phone and scheduled an appointment for next week. Thursday, at 9:00. He made a neat entry in his calendar.

He turned to the work files on his desk. If he was losing his mind, what difference did any of it make? The thought shocked him—he never had such thoughts. He should get some coffee. He always had one coffee a day. In the morning. But other people drank coffee throughout the day. "I need a pick-me-up," they said.

Downstairs at the coffee shop, there was no one in line. A young Hispanic girl stood behind the counter of the coffee shop, cleaning a machine. She must be new. He cleared his throat; she turned and approached.

"May I help you, sir?"

"Uh, yes. An Americano. Where is Susan?"

She turned to the coffee machine. "Who?"

"Susan. The usual barista. Or Mohammed."

She shook her head. "I don't know them. I just started last week. Parson Peterman. The only other barista is Harrison."

He flinched. "Parsons Peterman? The accountant on the 7th floor?"

She filled the cup. "I...I don't think so. He's the owner and manager. My dad knows him, it's how I got the job."

Why would Parsons buy the coffee shop?

When was he in here last? Wasn't it just a couple of days ago? He had seen Susan. She gave him his coffee!

The girl set his Americano on the counter. He paid and turned away.

Something was plainly wrong with him. He should go home. But he returned to his office. Kailee was coming from the back as he entered.

"Kailee? Do you know anything about Parson buying the downstairs coffee shop?"

"Who?"

"The coffee shop downstairs. The one that was—"

"I know the coffee shop. Who did you say bought it?"

"Well, I don't know for sure, but the girl said Parson bought it."

"Who's that?"

"Who's what?"

"Parson. Who's that?"

•••

Charlie ran into the parking lot. He'd drive himself to the hospital. It would be okay.

His car was gone.

Maybe not. Maybe, in his distraction, he'd parked it somewhere else, though he always parked in the same spot. He always arrived at 7:45 so he could park close to the building and in the shade. There was another car in that spot. A silver-gray Torino. About five or six years old.

He ran from one side of the parking lot to the other, but his car was not here.

What if he didn't remember what it looked like?

He tried to calm his heart. Inside the building lobby, he caught his breath and approached the desk.

"Good afternoon, Mr. Chesterton," Barclay said. "Are you okay?"

"Yes, yes, Barclay. Do you have any idea where my car is?"

"Your car?"

Charlie sighed. "I know you aren't responsible for the parking lot. But there are guards and cameras, right? Because my car is missing."

"I…didn't know you had a car, sir. You always take the bus. Did you drive it today?"

His heart pounded. "I take the bus? To work?"

"Yes. You complain when it is late because you like to arrive each day at 7:45. For coffee. He peered at him. "Mr. Chesterton, you don't look well. Sit down over there and let me call someone."

Charlie shook his head, backing out of the building. "No, no…I'm fine."

He turned and ran.

•••

He got off the bus three blocks from his house. Nothing about the bus was familiar. He didn't know the fare. Yet the bus driver called him by name, and when he asked how much it was, she laughed like it was a joke. When she saw he was not amused, she told him to to scan his pass. She insisted he had one, and when he took out his wallet, he found a Raleigh City Transit Pass card.

He burst through the front door calling for Cynthia, running through the house to find her. She was not downstairs. He bolted upstairs, still calling her name, but he already feared she was not home. Maybe he should call 911.

She was not in the bedroom or the bathroom. Empty. As he turned to leave, he jerked to a stop. Her closet was partially open, and inside he saw a hanging suit.

He approached with careful steps and slid the door open. A row of men's dress and semi-dress clothes. His style, but he recognized none of them. Light-headed, he walked over to his closet. More men's clothes. Casual, exercise. Some he recognized, but most he did not.

He plopped down on the bed, head in hands. His heart was hammering, his chest aching. He needed help. Breathe. Breathe. It's a panic attack.

Is this what it was like to lose one's mind? How dementia patients experience life? What it felt like before one died?

"No!" he said aloud, jumping to his feet. He would *not* give in. He would get help, whatever that meant. What was that movie where the guy was crazy, but he fought through it, teaching himself not to believe his own mind? That was it—*A Beautiful Mind*. He could do that.

What if it was a tumor? Well…he'd fight that too. Get the best doctors.

The first step was to get to the hospital. Call 911. He rushed down the stairs, taking them two at a time, into the living room and skidded to a halt.

The living room decor was unrecognizable. A sort of Classic Oriental. Not the Americana that he and Cynthia preferred.

He had *just been down here*. It wasn't like this ten minutes ago.

Was it?

He bolted into the kitchen and pulled open the drawer where they kept the bills. Rifling through them, he looked at the addressee on each. "Charles Chesterton." But none had Cynthia's name. They should have.

He turned to the cupboard. Her recipe box. With handwritten recipes.

There it was! Trembling, he opened the lid. The cards were all there, but it was not her handwriting. He didn't recognize it.

His head pounded and his heart felt like it would burst out of his chest. He screamed and ran out the front door. Across the way, a man he did not recognize was getting mail out of Jim's mailbox.

"Hey! Hey! What are you doing?"

The man turned around and laughed. "Getting my mail, Charlie. What are you doing?"

"Where's Jim?!"

"Jim? Who's Jim? Are you okay?"

"Jim! Jim! *Jim!* Lived there for seven years!" Charlie pointed at the house.

The man snorted. "Are you drunk, pal? Gone off the wagon?" He had been walking towards Charlie as they talked and as he drew near, he sobered. "Charlie, what's wrong? You don't look okay."

"*Stop it!*" Charlie yelled, spitting. "Who are you and what did you do with Jim?!"

"Hey, calm down, calm down. Charlie, Charlie, I've lived here for four years. You know that. Let's go inside, let me call—"

"Get away!" Charlie spun and ran back toward his house, tripping over the curb. He sprawled on the gravel of his front yard.

Gravel? There was no gravel in his front yard.

He raised up and came to his feet. His mouth dropped open. In the place of his ranch-style home was a mobile home. Perched on a foundation. Flowers and shrubs were planted all along its base, and a curving walkway, made of bricks, ran through the gravel yard. Step by step, he approached the door. Crunch. Crunch. Crunch.

He clumped the steps and opened the door.

The living room of a sparsely furnished modern mobile home. IKEA, from the looks of it all.

He turned back to the man who was not Jim standing in the road. It was a woman. Large. Blonde.

"Charlie?" She shouted. "Are you okay? Let me call Peter."

THREE HOURS AND
THIRTEEN MINUTES

12:16 pm

"This will teach you!" I screamed in the small, dark space. My eyes grew dim with exertion. "I hope you feel so bad you kill yourself."

My head banged against something. All I could see were dim reflections of flotsam in the water.

I spit salt water and vomited.

11:41 am

I didn't hear the engine cut off because of the screaming wind and booming waves. The wheel became unresponsive, and my first thought was of a broken rudder or hydraulic line. Then I saw the black RPM gauge was at zero. Faulty gauge? I pulled back on the throttle and then shoved it forward. No response.

The next wave lifted the boat and began to turn it sideways. Up over the crest of the big wave, then down at a 45-degree angle.

I cursed at Mike. I *just* had him check the systems two weeks ago: filters, hoses, fluids, gauges—all of it. This was not a good reflection on him—I pay a lot to make sure things like this don't happen.

"You're fired when I get back!"

11:15 am

Three miles out. The swells were close to six feet, walls of water that made it rough going. But it was the chop that made it so difficult to keep control of the wheel and stay on course. My stomach was tight, and my shoulders sore from hunching. Still, I'd been out in similar conditions before. Once, anyway. Coming back from San Lucas with Paul. Five years ago. The squall hit when we were eight miles out. It was my first time in severe weather. I thought we were going to capsize, so I left the helm to get the emergency equipment. Paul stopped me with a dark look and a single word. He took the waves at an angle, played the throttle like a violin, and got us to port.

At a party later, he told everyone back home that I panicked. I didn't panic—I was being safe. I was going to get out the gear—the PFDs, flares, EPIRB, hand-held—and have it ready just in case. Then I would go back to the helm and get us in. Taking precautions. Which is the smart thing to do. But that's not the story he told. So I threw the beer in his face and left the party. Don't need friends like that.

I was gripping the wheel too tight. I forced myself to relax. *If only you could see me, Beth! You'd be scared for me, and you'd apologize, and beg me to come back in with tears streaming down your face!*

She knew I was going to the marina today after our fight, and could guess I'd take the boat out. Surely she'd be worried when it started to rain. She'd check the weather. Then she'd feel guilty. I smiled.

A lurch and bang brought my attention back. I'd just reached the bottom of the trough between two waves, at the safe angle, but the wave was so steep the bowsprit dug into the water and then reared back up, reflecting the water over the bow and back, drenching me where I stood. The cold wetness took my breath away. I was blind for a moment.

What was that sound? Something must have fallen or broken loose. I look around the helm, and down behind me onto the aft cockpit. Nothing I could see. Maybe something inside the cabin.

I wished I'd bought an autopilot last month. Even that cheap one I saw. Set it at about 60 degrees perpendicular to the waves, then I could go down to check. Not for long in these conditions, but for a little. Without one, I could not leave the wheel. Waves would turn her sideways within seconds. Being hit broadside with wind and water this strong was a sure way to capsize.

An alarm sounded. The oil pressure. Was I running her that hard? No, only 10 knots. But it was all down-hill. Worse than the time with Paul.

I got a little scared. Should I turn back?

I reflected on the trip with Paul and thought "no." I was smart and tough. Besides, if I went in now, she might never know how bad it was out here.

Another two or three miles out, then turn back. That would make it about ten from shore. That should do it.

Wish I had some way of knowing if she'd checked the marine weather yet.

11:51 am

I spun the wheel to starboard. That should help, even without engines, but with the power of oncoming wind and waves, it wouldn't last long. The vessel would begin to turn sideways and take the waves broadside. I turned the key off, waited a moment, then turn the ignition. I couldn't hear anything. The gauge needles did not move.

We hit the trough, and the boat skidded a little to starboard. I looked ahead. The swells must be eight or nine feet now—taller than the boat save for the antenna. It approached like a green-white wall and turned the vessel sideways. I lost my footing as we canted, and I crashed into the port gunwale, my left ribcage taking the brunt against the gunwale. I gasped in pain. The boat listed to 45 degrees or more then started to come back.

I grabbed the console and pulled myself up, breathing hard with my face against the gauges. I raised up a bit, staring at the gauge before my eyes.

Fuel.

Empty.

I was so angry at her when I got to the dock, I didn't even check. She will really feel bad.

Pulling myself up by the wheel, I dropped my head back and screamed. At her. At Mike. At this insane world.

The boat rocked to starboard, up over the next crest, and back down. I spread my legs and gripped the console with all my might. The stern began to come around, and when we hit the trough, the vessel jerked as if a giant had reached down and slapped it. Water poured over gunwales, soaking me again.

10:15 am

"Hey, buddy, headed out?"

I finished untying the last line and jumped back aboard. I nodded as I took the wheel. His lips moved as he said something else, but I couldn't hear him over the engines.

I threw the throttle into reverse and left it low, backing out of the slip. Once clear of the finger piers, I shifted to neutral and let her drift, spinning the rudder so that the stern moved to starboard. As I waited, I looked back at the pier. He had his hands cupped around his mouth. Was he blind? He knew I couldn't hear him from this distance with engines running. I waved.

Shifting into forward, I left the marina behind at just under 5 knots. It took only about 10 minutes to get to the entrance of the ocean. I was surprised at the size of the swells and the wind, and the horizon was dark with clouds. The wind was about 18 knots, maybe. It was always worse near the entrance. Right into the mouth like a funnel. I rarely took her out anywhere above 18, but I needed to get away today. Besides, I was sick of her ridiculous demands. I screamed a profanity as loud as I could. It felt great. It's what I like about going out on the boat. No one could hear you or judge you.

12:03 pm

I reached for the radio, flipped up the little red cover, and pushed the button. A red light flashed.

The boat rocked to starboard so far I was sure we'd capsize. To my left, the churning water seemed only inches from my face. The vessel righted itself, then went over the port almost as far, and back again. I watched as the next swell approached. It looked ten feet high.

The radio lit up.

"Vessel signaling emergency, vessel signaling emergency, what is your emergency? Coast Guard Santa Cruz, over."

I grabbed the mic and squeezed. "Coast Guard Santa Cruz, this is the *Dark Reflection* out of Santa Cruz. I'm out of fuel. Conditions—"

I lost the mic as another crash brought me to the deck. A wave of water slapped me like a wet blanket as I lay. I scrambled back up, grabbed the radio cable, and found the mic. "In danger of capsizing—over."

"*Dark Reflection*, We have your GPS location from your radio. Scrambling a cutter now. What is the size of your vessel, color, markings? Over."

"22 -foot single engine. White with red trim. Over."

"Affirmative, *Dark Reflection*. Are you taking on water? Over."

"I…I don't know. Rocking over 60 degrees back and forth." I didn't think that was an exaggeration. "Over."

Silence. Then a new voice.

"Copy that, CGSC. On our way. What's the idiot doing out in this—"

"—watch the chatter, Cutter Five. Over"

"Sorry, CGSC. We are top speed to coordinates. ETA, 30 minutes. Pretty nasty out here. Over."

"Affirmative. *Dark Reflection*, are you in immediate danger of life? Over."

I looked about. There was water on the bridge and in the aft cockpit. Could just be from the waves. I should check the cabin belowdecks.

"Coast Guard, not sure. Some water, lot of wave action. Over."

"*Dark Reflection*, advise you put on a life jacket or an survival suit if you have one. Grab flotation devices, go to an open area of the boat that you can abandon quickly. Do you have EPIRB or portable radio? Over."

"Yes, both. Going to get them." Already had my life jacket out. Did he think I was an idiot?

The next swell knocked me down again, and I slid down the short ladder into the aft cockpit.

9:03 am

"You are being irrational!"

"That's your go-to insult whenever I'm winning the argument." I tried to keep my voice down in contrast to her squealing.

She let out an explosive sigh. "God, Tunny, you are so exasperating!"

"Yeah? Well, what would you do?"

"I'd stay! So what if they moved you to a new department? They gave you a raise! There's more room for advancement. They said—"

"So it's all about the money for you?"

I saw the hurt in her eyes. Good. Knew that would strike home after that argument last month about our respective salaries. "You're missing the point, as usual. I've been with this company for twelve years! Exceptional employee, won sales awards half of those years. *Everyone* tells me how good I am. So why do they want to move me to administration? I'm not a suit. I don't want to be one. I want to sell! They took my commissions away!"

"Because you'll be making more money, and it's guaranteed money! Why can't you see this is a promotion?"

"Because it *isn't*. This is all Tanya's doing. She hates me."

She rolled her eyes. I wanted to punch her. "Why would she hate you? You don't even sell to the same regions."

"She's jealous of my sales. And she sucks up to the suits all the time. She wears those low-cut dresses, and those idiots don't see she's playing them."

She threw up her hands and turned away. "So it's reverse sexism now? I give up."

"You are so stupid! It's not sexism. It's about taking away everything I love!" I had lost the battle against raising my voice.

She turned back and cocked her head. "Everything?"

I slammed my fist down on the table and swore. "What is it with you?!

She stepped forward. "You're so blind! Anyone else would see this as a reward for all those years you had to work like crazy to make a decent living on commissions. You did it well, so they want to reward you by putting you in *charge* of sales, and teaching others how to do it!"

I laughed in her face. "Yeah. That's what *they* said. Figures you'd take their side."

"Because it's true! Aaargh!" she turned away again, head down. "I swear, Tunny, sometimes I think you have no ability to reflect on anything with logic and clarity.

I stood up, knocking over the chair and spilling a glass of water. "Yeah? Well, sometimes I think you have no ability to be supportive. Three years, and you are *still* taking everyone else's side." I grabbed my keys from the table and stormed past. Her eyes were wide, her mouth open. I threw open the door, making sure it slammed against the opposite wall.

"Where are you going? Don't leave, Tunny!"

"The boat! Go to hell!"

12:11 pm

I half crawled and half slid to the entrance to the below cabin. Grabbing the handholds on either side of the bulkhead, I took one step at a time down the cabin and stepped into about a foot of water. As I fumbled for the light switch, another jerk of the boat knocked me down.

I pulled myself over to the port storage compartments. Being inside the cabin was far worse, like an angry giant was shaking the boat back and forth. Unclasping the lock, I groped inside and found the **EPIRB**. The portable radio was on its charger in front of the little galley. I found it without trouble and headed back to the bulkhead, tottering and sloshing like a drunk man.

At the stairs, I clipped the radio to my belt and shoved the **EPIRB** into my pants pocket

She knows how much this boat means to me. If I lose it, she'll feel responsible. I smiled at the prospect of her pleading "Oh Tunny, I am so sorry, it is all my fault. I am just so glad you are alive. I'll never—"

The world exploded in violence. I went head over heels with water, appliances, bottles—*stuff*—all flying as if that giant had just flung the boat through the air.

It was dark. The water was so cold. The shock felt like a heart attack. So much dark water. Did I fall overboard?

I kept banging my arms, legs, head, on hard objects. I reach out and felt solid objects. Something was swirling around my right leg, and it hurt so bad. Did a shark bite me?

No. I was still in the cabin. A cabin filled with water. Dark reflections rolling, rocking, banging. Every item in the cabin, including me, was sloshing around like we were in a washing machine.

My head was above water. I reached up and smacked a surface. Flat. Hard. It made no sense. The roof of the cabin was a soft upholstery. I kicked with my legs and one arm, moving the opposite hand on the hard surface. It hurt my side and leg to move. *Where am I?*

My hand smacked another object. A post. I grasped it and slid my hand down, following it into the cold water. About three feet down it met a hard, horizontal surface.

I ducked my head under and felt along it. It was long and flat.

I was in a strange place. Somewhere other than my boat. Disoriented. I felt underneath the fixed object. It had a ridge, running all around—

It was the table. The table beside the galley. Upside down.

The boat has capsized.

I shot back out of the water and hit my head on the roof. Or rather, the deck floor. My heart pounded in my chest. My feet and legs were numb. My breath would come. Was the space running out of oxygen?

Where was the bulkhead opening?

Is this what panic feels like? Or hypothermia?

Or death?

God damn her to hell! If she hadn't been so selfish, so mean—

My leg hit something sharp and I cried out.

Was the air space getting smaller?

I swam about, trying to feel along the edges. Trying to find something familiar that could orient me. *Where was the bulkhead out of this cabin?!*

The air space *was* getting smaller. With my mouth out of the water, my head touched the roof. Deck. I flailed. The opening had to be somewhere. *The cabin is not that big!*

I dove, swimming along the edges of this dark space. Hands scrabbling about, feeling for an opening. Things kept banging into my arms as they flailed.

Out of air, I surfaced. I had to lean my head back to breathe. *This is all your fault.* I smelled the coppery odor of blood. My leg was surely broken. Probably my ribs, too.

"This will teach you!" I screamed in the small, dark space. My eyes grew dim with exertion. "I hope you feel so bad you kill yourself."

My head banged against something. All I could see were dim reflections of flotsam in the water.

I spit salt water and vomited.

RINGING

Room spinning grab chair back lean on bar look around no one saw clumsy

Ringing no beeping beeping but ringing phone where here in pocket

"Hello?

"Jason?"

"Mom." Sound normal can't let mom known how much too much how many speak slow

"Where are you? I thought you were coming home at four-thirty?"

"No. Was going to, but got caught with—"bartender looking over here no looking to right two people man and woman older people married? maybe hope not really pretty woman

"Jason?"

"Sorry mom talking to people here in…in…in meeting. Went longer than I thought." Slow down is it slurred don't let mom know how much got to pee got to sound normal

"Are you okay, Jason? You sound funny."

"Yes. Yes. Just busy here at the conference."

"I hate it when you go to these conferences. I don't know why you stay at the hotel when our house is only forty minutes away. When will you be home? I need you here. You told me you'd be home at four-thirty after the conference ended. You said today was the last day."

Nag nagger complain complainer grit teeth leave alone keep it together never win

"I'll be there when I get there. Last meeting is going late and then we're going to dinner." Breathe slow talking too fast or mom will figure it out. "Don't tell me what to do, mom, I'm a grown man forty years—"

"Now Jason, do not talk to me that way. You still live with me and I am—" snap phone close in pocket feel bad will ring again don't care look sideways did man and woman hear? no man and woman talking a lot laughing wish could be happy too so pretty blonde nice tan dressed nice

"Bartender. Bartender! What's your name?"

"I'm Devon."

"Well, Devon, I wanna buy them two a round. Round of drinks. On me."

"These two, sir?" Pointing man and woman is pretty maybe not married maybe just met here talking

"Yes. Round of drinks for them. On me. They are so happy don'tcha think?"

"Sure thing." Goes over can't hear how nice eyes meet then back silence ugly stupid just trying to be nice

Man looks here "Thank you, that's very kind of you." Looks rich nice woman says something can't hear but smiling good should go talk to woman get up not yet wait for drink

Bartender watching eyebrows raised looks back at man and woman

"Gin and tonic with Hendricks? And you ma'am?"

"Dirty martini, please."

Man turns back looks probably same age but better why can't look like that been kept down

"Thank you again, sir."

Nod say something don't know woman pretty wonder if married? hope not should go talk get up careful bar stool room spins slow these are good people "I'm gonna go over and talk to her." Keep hand on chairs past man past woman pull chair too high think stupid ugly no seems nice maybe attractive have good job "You seem very happy and very pretty."

"Thank you. And thank you for the drink." Smile pretty eyes nice maybe different

"You're welcome." What to do? don't know turns away bartender looks at man makes funny face what is it? people talking stupid ringing no beeping but ringing phone beeping mom again take it out hang up mom ruins everything look back no one looking no one loves back never did but maybe someone

"Where are you from?" woman blonde classy have to pee get up everyone looks woman looks at bartende get up slow hold chair back hear whisper behind had five Manhattans conference people went to dinner left here sad turn right step step hard to walk step step its upstairs yes step step bright

drop phone floor tilts almost fell got it got it in pocket on way to men's room in corner wobble must be worse than thought mom is stupid am grown man job divorced hated oh right turn push door go in

"Excuse me." Move past black shirt white dots employee where is urin-urin-urinal ok much better should have come sooner wonder is woman attracted to—have good job should lose weight but bought drinks other guy looks better maybe married wonder so happy

Zip up zip up not washing hands door open old man gray beard smiles go past such a large area so many windows bright but it's night watch stairs pretty drunk maybe can handle it, step, step at chair sit wave to bartender "Jack and coke, good ma'am?" Different bartender older pretty long black hair nods "And 'nother round for my friends here" bartender grabs more glasses "the happy ones right here" pointing so bartender knows woman is pretty get back up "Okay I am going to go over here" to bartender all watching go to sit next to pretty woman no stumbling should ask don't be forward all looking like waiting for good speech or funny joke

Woman looking no speaking "Are…are you married, ma'am?"

Looks at man looks back smiles back what

"I just…you are very pretty are you happy?"

She smiles. "Yes, I'm happy."

That is so nice nod say so nice not really but could be ringing no beeping beeping but ringing phone beeping

"Hello?"

"Jason, do not *ever* hang up on me again."

"I know mom very sorry" ruins everything bought drinks nice "just very busy and you are making it hard to do my job—"

"You aren't at your job, Jason. It's night."

"Dinner here, mom. I told you…going out to dinner. At this place and now it's everyone after talking and eating and going over the day I'll be home when i get home." Anger too much mom will figure out five Manhattans and what jack and coke and something else

"Jason, dear, I am not trying to be difficult. I know you work hard. I love you and want you to be okay. You need some good rest—I know how those conferences wear you out."

"I'm okay. Have to work and do this then be home." Slurring too much slow down don't need mom telling talking never stops talking don't understand anything mumble yes yes yes

"Okay. I'm just being supportive like a good mom should. Text me when you leave?"

"Yes, mom. Will text."

So irritating why has this happened even kids don't care dropped daughter off at college all daughter wanted was money didn't say thanks dad but mom poisons mind but woman and man new friends wave to bartender

"I'd like to buy them drinks. They seem nice and happy, huh?"

Bartender looks and stares and looks. "Yes, yes they are."

Nods goes to bar look at man woman looking over here "Are you married?"

"Yes, yes we are." Man spoke woman looks at man back here back at man back here funny look

"Are you happy?"

"We are very happy."

Oh so wonderful so good want to be happy but mom's fault drove off last date

"I gotta come over here." Get up be careful with drink don't want to be ſtupid drunk walk paſt woman paſt man hand on shoulder sit next to man

"That is great so why are you two arguing?" Look at man is blurry focus focus

"We aren't arguing. Every relationship has ſtuff. I juſt think she gets up too early in the morning. But really, that's no big deal because I love her. We juſt talk about it sometimes."

Looks at woman looks at man looks over again funny look

"Do you love him?" Woman turns and funny look maybe too personal should not have asked no is okay very pretty

"Yes, I love him very much." Funny look again what is it something ſtupid *ſtupid*

So wonderful. "So wonderful. Let me buy drinks." Where is bartender what was name different one wave "more drinks on me" so tired so tired these are good people wish wasn't married muſt go pee again get up careful

Stairs loſt shoe it's a flip flop funny name flip flop flop flip where is it where is it back down bend over clackity clack oh phone again never mind don't care back up ſtairs

Wait where is it it's outside through glass what oh, sneezing and sneezing can't ſtand bend over sneeze ſtand up woozy another funny word woozy boozy should go back to pretty woman yes ſtairs going down wait bar is backward everything is flipped

"Sir, can I help you?"

Who is it white shirt small woman waiter no don't remember

"Sir, what room are you staying in?"

"Who are *you*?"

"I'm the manager." Manager or something of bar or hotel remember now saw when first here

"Sir what room are you staying it?"

"In, in 6798, it's up there." Wave to upper floors manager should know

"What is your last name?" Why name? not pretty not interested liked the other so nice so pretty but married

"Are you ready to go to your room? You have had a lot of fun tonight, but maybe it's time to call it a day."

Lot of fun yes not conference people but nice married people happy want to be happy all mom's fault drives everyone away

"Would you like some help, sir? I can get someone to help you to your room."

Nice lady trying to help knows good time not like mom not bossy "No, 'm fine thank you." Look up look over

"The elevators are there." Pointing yes, remember go over push button man alongside uniform conference guy no not conference guy maybe bell…bell…who?… bellhop another funny word bell dell nell hop drop top

"Hello, sir. How are you?"

Nodding nodding "Hello. It is good night *yes*."

"Yes it is, sir. Are you going up?"

"Yes, time to go to bed. Don't want to."

"But it is late."

Doors open didn't hear open man motions go in.

"May I press the button for you, sir? What room are you in?"

Nice man such nice happy people

"6798."

"Actually, I believe it is 6789, isn't it? Your name is Jason?"

Oh knows me? wonder if woman told man or maybe pretty woman or not or man or maybe is from conference? no belly hoppy that's funny laughing smiles back nice

"Yes, yes, my name's Jason, nice to meet you."

"Nice to meet you, sir."

Doors close elevator spinning hold rail lean on wall look around anyone see? just nice man here pushed button nice wonder which room pretty woman married woman wish

"Here we are at your floor, May I help you to your room?"

Stumble carpet tripped don't feel good not good sick at door man opens where did key come from it's okay inside now need to lay down bed room spinning grab chair back lean on bar look around anyone see that no alone just—

Ringing no beeping beeping but ringing ringing ringing

HATS

The man had no hat.

He disappeared around the corner before Ponti could get a second look. Pulling his jacket collar high and scrunched down his head, Ponti ran to the corner, just in time to see the man turn the next corner.

He was right. No hat.

He resisted the urge to run down the street to that corner. There were too many people about, and he was conspicuous enough. A quick turn about brought him face-to-face with a man and woman coming the other way. An apologetic smile began on their faces, then froze. Averting their eyes and scooting past.

Ponti hunched his jacket higher and continued towards home. He dreaded these weekly excursions, but he needed groceries, and Sturb's Market was closest. Milford's was bigger, and not too much farther, but they did not allow him to shop there. The next closest was over four miles away.

Thankfully, it was one of the few times he had to leave his apartment. "You should be thankful it's so close," the social worker had told him.

That man walked as if he didn't care. How did he manage that?

•••

As he put away the groceries, he imagined himself in the store, head up, jacket hanging loose around his body. Head held high. Meeting the eyes of strangers.

It seemed scandalous. How would the clerk react? The clerk had never made eye contact with Ponti. Hundreds of visits and the man had never so much as glanced at Ponti's face.

He walked back through his little apartment to the front door, to stand in front of the hat rack affixed to the wall. The social worker told him not to remove it under penalty of law. Was that indeed a law? How would they know? He sighed. He was not one to take chances.

At his chair in the living room, he eschewed his usual book-reading to sit and think. Who was that man? Where had he been going?

After a few moments, Ponti jumped up and ran to the kitchen. Pawing through the trash bin, he located the receipt from Sturb's. It was too dark to read. He went to the door, holding the slip of paper up to the gray light filtering in through the small window near the top.

"Check out: 3:35 PM." He figured it took fifteen minutes to shop and check out. Five minutes to walk from the market from the corner? About right. So the man had turned the corner around 3:15.

He looked at the door. He only opened it once a week most weeks. But there was no law that said he couldn't open it more often.

•••

Three days. Three days of standing across the street between 2:00 and 2:30. He couldn't stand more than thirty minutes. The stares. The avoidance. Words under their breath. Once, a kid even yelled at him. He didn't hear what he said, but the other kids burst into laughter.

On the first day, he stood between a bookstore and a tile supply showroom. When the bookstore owner told him to leave, he moved to the corner of an alley beside an electronics supply store. After about ten minutes, an employee came out.

"What are you doing there?"

"I'm…I'm waiting for someone."

She glanced up and away with a frown.

"I'm sorry. I'll only be here for thirty minutes, just a few days."

She shook her head and looked back at the store.

"Okay. Just…just try to stay back."

"Yes, yes…thank you."

She left.

On this third day, no one bothered him. He discovered that he could stand just behind in the alley entrance, behind a large trash bin, and still see the corner across the street. If anyone saw him, or someone came up from behind, it would appear suspicious. But he would not be here long or—

There he was!

Walking down the middle of the sidewalk. Hands in the pockets of his coat.

Bareheaded.

The man looked neither right nor left. Others averted their eyes, stared, or muttered. He paid no attention, as if he didn't care. As if it didn't matter.

Ponti moved away from the bin and crossed the street, almost forgetting to watch for traffic. He had his large coat on, the one with the big collar. Pulled up high. Head down, but eyes looking up.

The man turned the corner, and Ponti turned behind him. How strange it must look. Two of them, one right behind the other, out in the open. He pushed aside the anxiety and matched the man's pace. Five yards.

He turned the second corner—the same one the man had turned three days ago, and Ponti followed. He did his best to ignore the stares and comments.

They approached a cross street. A lot of traffic and people. He can't lose him. Not having come this far. The man turned into a narrow alley just before the busy street, catching Ponti off-guard. He sped up and turn the corner—

And came face to face with the man.

"Are you following me?!" The man had his hands balled into fists, held low.

Ponti stepped back. "I…I…"

They stood staring at each other for a frozen moment. The man relaxed his hands and dropped his shoulders. "I know." He beckoned with his head. "Follow me."

He turned and walked away without looking back. Ponti stood for a moment, looked right and left, then followed. He supposed the man might try to rob him or beat him up, but surely he knew he had nothing of worth.

They entered a small close. Old brick buildings. Trash in the corners and a musty, ancient smell. Cooler here than out on the street. Across the close, a wooden door stood ajar. A door that someone had painted long ago, now faded and peeling.

The man stopped and turned toward him. Flecks of gray hair and wrinkles. Sad eyes that contrasted with his bold demeanor.

"I don't have to tell you to keep quiet about this place."

"What is it?"

"You'll see. If you enter with me."

Ponti's curiosity got the better of him.

•••

Twelve men sat in a circle. Some on folding chairs, some on crates. They ranged from their early twenties to late sixties or older. All dressed in shabby cloths. Like Ponti.

And like Ponti, none had hats.

There had been consternation when Ponti entered, but the man who brought him assured them he was no problem. They took their places, and a man called "Jukes" spoke. He told of a cabbie who kicked him out of his cab when he ducked in the car. Next, the man to the right of Jukes spoke. A young woman in the street had screamed at him to get away from her little boy.

They continued around the circle, each relating a story of abuse. A few were worse than anything Ponti had experienced. The police arrested an older man and jailed him for three days, accusing him of robbery. They kept him until the CCTV footage showed he had not even entered the store.

The man who brought him was next: his name was Edward. He related how difficult it was for him to change telephone providers. When finished, he nodded to Ponti.

Ponti had never talked about his experiences. For the last eight years, he had spoken to no one except for necessary social interactions—groceries, supplies, and meetings with the social worker. Work interactions took place through electronic messages, all from home.

"I...I was standing on the sidewalk. Enjoying the fresh air. A—a few days ago. The owner of a nearby store told me to move away from his store." He stopped, unsure of how much more to say. Jukes rescued him by indicating the man next to him.

The rest finished. Jukes spoke again.

"I have some promising news. I told you of the man I met a short while back, a government official and well-off. As I told you, I was surprised how he spoke to me when we met outside the courthouse. As if he didn't notice."

He paused. A few of the others nodded their heads.

"We met again two days ago. He said he used to be one of us."

Exclamations and murmurs erupted from the group. Jukes waited, nodding. Someone said, "How is that even possible?"

"I don't know. But he spoke about a movement, an idea, to change all this. There are a group of officials who feel the same. They'd approached others, and while many refused to listen, and some threatened him, a few agreed with him. He said many women were tentatively supportive, and that—"

"Of course the women are!" Edward exclaimed. "They have nothing to lose. If *they* had to—"

Jukes held up a hand. "We've talked that issue to death, Edward. And it isn't the point."

Another spoke up. "What *is* the point?"

"He wants us to tell him our stories. Just like we do here. Write them down and give them to him."

An explosion of protestations. "I don't know…" "What for?!" "So they can use them against us?" "Write them *down?*"

Jukes held up a hand again, and once more, commanded silence. "He wants to give a face to our problem. Real stories. Human stories."

There was silence. Ponti looked around the room. It all seemed so unreal. There was a…a *support* group? He would not have imagined it was allowed. And they had ideas of *change?* It was both exciting and terrifying.

There was a commotion outside the door. Jukes stood up as everyone turned. The door slammed open against the wall. Black-dressed figures, masked, scrambled in, shouting and gesturing with rifles. No, not rifles. Bats. Pipes.

Chairs flew and crates scraped across the floor as the circle broke and the men ran for the opposite door. Ponti froze as every old fear broke upon him. The first man reached the opposite door just as it crashed open, knocking him back. To Ponti's right, one intruder swung his bat, catching Jukes on his side. He went down with a scream. Many of the members now turned to fight back. Fists and chairs against bats and pipes.

Ponti scrambled backward out of his chair and fell with a crash. He crab-crawled to the nearest wall as two men, locked in battle, flew past. He scrunched against the wall. It was like a riot in a room, a bar brawl in a movie, a gang war in a warehouse.

The opposite door was clear. He scrambled sideways, keeping his back against the wall, to the far corner and then towards the doorway. Ten more feet. He rose to run.

A heavy mass crashed into him from behind. Two others, writhing and bashing each other. He could not breathe. He struggled to drag himself out from under. They rolled away: two men, fists pummeling at close range.

Ponti got to his hands and knees. Caught his breath. Looked up.

A hat lay on the floor.

Cheap. Black. Crumpled.

He looked at the door.

With a single motion, he came to his feet, grabbed the hat and ran. Out the door. Another alley. Narrow. Dim. Tall buildings. A light at the end. Cars flashing.

He sprinted to the light.

•••

Ponti walked into Milford's Groceries. Much larger than Sturb's. Many more choices. Along with his usual items, he chose a rather expensive bottle of wine and some imported cheese.

He joined the line at the checkout counter. As he waited, he perused the magazine and newspaper stand beside the line.

The woman in front of him pointed at a daily newspaper. "Can you believe it?"

Vigilante Group Breaks Up Secret Meeting

Ponti shook his head. "No. What were they thinking?"

She pursed her lips. "What did they expect? Meeting like that."

"Up to no good, I'm sure."

She nodded. "Well, they got what they deserved."

Ponti smiled. "Indeed."

PREPARATION

"I don't know why you enjoy picking up the bodies with me."

"Why wouldn't I?"

Peter shrugged. "Well, it isn't your job. It's Mickey or Pablo's job. But also because it's weird. It's what U get paid to do, but I wouldn't volunteer."

"Mickey and Pablo aren't available. Besides, I like it."

"See? That's weird. We're picking up a dead body and taking it to the mortuary. No one should like that."

"Well, maybe 'like' is not the right word. It satisfies me. It's important."

Peter shook his head. "You're the embalming assistant. You don't have to go pick up the bodies."

Morty shrugged. He didn't see what was so strange providing a service to the dead and their survivors. People who had experienced loss and devastation. That's a good thing to do.

They pulled in front of the house. Peter checked the address in his notebook, then went to the door. Morty watched as he spoke to the woman who answered. He imagined somber tones. Hands folded in front. Small nods of the head. A sympathetic expression.

Peter waved at him to come. The woman led them into a dark bedroom. The old man lay on the bed, a sheet and blanket pulled up to his chin. The familiar grayish pallor; the mouth hanging slightly open.

"Ma'am," Peter said, in dulcet tones, "are you the next-of-kin?"

"Yes, I'm his sister."

"No spouse or child?"

"No, not in the area. They'll be here late tonight. Does that matter?"

"No, not at all. I just need a next-of-kin for the paperwork. Is there somewhere we can sit and go over the paperwork?"

While Peter dealt with that, Morty returned to the Toyota Hiace. He pulled the collapsible stretcher from the hearse and extended the legs. From the back, he took a folded bag and the medical bag, placing it on the stretcher. He pulled it into the house.

Setting the medical bag on the floor, he unfolded the black bag on the stretcher and unzipped it. He spread it open, like a flayed fish, ready for the body. From the bag, he took two pairs of gloves and laid them next to each other. A clipboard with a form to list valuables and clothing completed his preparation.

He stood beside the body. So fascinating. One moment there was breath, motion (even if imperceptible). Blood flowing, heart beating (even if just barely), and synapses firing. Then it all stopped, like a complex machine that had been turned off and was winding down. The electricity stops. The fluids run down to the lowest point or back into the tanks. Gasses cause the stomach to bloat. He could already smell that distinctive odor—urine and defecation and the beginning of decomposition. A once vibrant and useful machine relegated to a static arrangement of parts.

Peter entered. "No communicable diseases. Hospice reported heart failure and filled out the pronouncement of death. No pacemaker. We'll return the clothes to them, they'll bring a suit to the mortuary. Ready?"

"Ready."

They pulled on their gloves. It was easy and always the same, with only minor variations because of the size and condition of the body. Morty had worked at the mortuary for fifteen years—first doing pickups, then, about nine years ago, assisting the embalmer. He'd helped with funeral arrangements, but found it boring. More enjoyable was the preparation for cremation, which he had done a few times. He helped with a few preparations for burials at sea. The manager had offered to pay for embalmer training, but Morty declined. If he became an embalmer, that's all he would do. He liked having a hand in all aspects.

Peter pulled the blankets and sheets back, folding them until the body was fully exposed. He looked up at Morty.

"Ready?"

Morty took up the clipboard and pen. "Go."

Peter worked his way from the top of the man's head to his toes, calling out each "valuable." There were only two: a watch and a wedding ring. As he called out each one, he placed it in a plastic bag.

Next came clothing: a nightshirt, a pair of loose underwear, and compression socks. Morty helped Peter remove the nightshirt by lifting the torso, then shoulders, so Peter could pull it over the man's head, then went back to the clipboard. Compression socks came next, also cataloged and bagged. The naked, shriveled, gray body lay before them, more like a mannequin than a human.

Morty maneuvered the stretcher next to the bed, and, at a nod, they lifted the corpse in one motion. Peter pulled the sheets and blankets back up and pulled them taut. He fluffed the pillows. "Essential," he always said, "nobody wants to come in and see the outline of their loved one's body left behind."

While he did that, Morty placed a thin pillow under the head to keep it raised. He made sure the torso was straight, legs together, and arms arranged with care. Taking the head in both hands and positioned it just so, he arranged the hair with a comb from his pocket for that purpose. He pushed the mouth shut as much as it would stay—the mortician would wire it shut later. He smiled: it was good work.

He zipped the bag while Peter reached under the stretcher and pulled the straps out and over the body, cinching them tight, but not too tight.

Each took an end, and they wheeled the stretcher through the house and out—feet first to avoid any purge from the mouth or nostrils. This last time his body would ever leave his home, Morty thought. A noble task entrusted to us.

Slow maneuvering down the three steps from the porch took skill. The family followed: the sister and two other adults. Once at the car, they slid the stretcher onto the lower shelf, its legs collapsing underneath like a football player having his legs cut out from under by an opponent.

Peter whispered to the family that they could say goodbye if they wished. He and Morty stood back at a respectable distance, hands clasped behind, heads bowed. A somber and meaningful moment. Two of the family approached and stood, looking at the black bag for a few moments. After they moved away, the the sister nodded at Peter.

As they drove, Morty said, "A job well done."

Peter didn't answer.

•••

"Will we be doing restoration?" Morty asked.

"No," Hidalgo said, "not this one."

Good. Morty didn't like restoration. He believed in the first three tenants of embalming: sanitization, presentation, and preservation. But restoration seemed insulting to him—because it wasn't restoration. It was play-acting. Using tricks of stage and taxidermy to pretend that the natural transition of the body had not taken place. It was an affront to nature.

"Did you prepare the injections?"

"Yes," Morty said. He picked up the tray of syringes and tubes and set it on the operations table beside the body. He'd often asked if he could perform the injections, but Hidalgo forbid it—"I could lose my license!"

He did allow Morty to perform the sanitation stage, because he had done it so many times with perfection. Hidalgo even allowed him to begin as soon as a body arrived, even if Hidalgo was not available. But he was forbidden from beginning the arterial and cavity embalming until the embalmer arrived. It frustrated Morty every time he sat and waited. This time, however, Hidalgo had already been at the mortuary when Peter and Morty arrived.

Sometimes, when Morty stayed late, he'd read the books in Hidalgo's office. It was a wonderful collection of works on anatomy, thanatology, and chemistry. Morty especially enjoyed the thick book describing the lives and works of William Harvey, William Hunter, August Wilhelm von Hofmann, and Frederic Ryusch. Men who had made a difference in the field; a field most people never thought about. Until they had too.

Hidalgo often asked why Morty didn't go for training. Morty would shrug and say, "Maybe someday."

The truth was, he'd spent almost ten years working with Hidalgo, and didn't want to waste his time studying something he already knew.

•••

No calls for three days. No bodies for embalming. A long and unusual stretch. Calls came almost every day—sometimes more than once.

Morty sat in the break room, staring at an empty coffee cup. Lea, the office secretary, came in. "Hey, Morty. What's up?"

"Nothing. Bored."

"You should try planning the ceremonies with Janine. Always busy."

"Done that. Nothing better than picking up bodies and prepping them."

She laughed as she poured the cup of coffee. "*Nothing better?*"

"No." He looked up. "I love it. What no one else will do. A job well done. That's where the fun is."

She shook her head. "Well, I get the 'job well done.' That's admirable. Not so sure how fun I'd find it." She turned to leave. "See you later."

She doesn't understand. I do stuff no one else will do. Like a hero, of sorts.

•••

A call finally came in late that night after he had gone home. Peter called, asking him if he wanted to go: Pablo was still on vacation and Mickey was not answering his phone.

Morty threw on his white shirt and black suit and drove to the mortuary.

"Didn't expect you for another fifteen minutes. Were you waiting, dressed already?"

Morty laughed. "No. Maybe I should."

Peter started the van.

This job was difficult. The deceased was a college-age kid who had overdosed. She was from a large family—children as young as three were running all about, oblivious to the import of the event. The police and medics had just finished their work. The mother's wails fill the home from another part of the house. While Peter dealt with the next-of-kin—the father—Morty set up in the kid's bedroom. The noise made it difficult to concentrate. Dignity was essential in these situations. The deceased deserved that, no matter how they died. Some people only thought of themselves.

However, Morty was a professional. He laid out the paraphernalia as it should be, prepared the stretcher, and checked over the body. Younger bodies had the gray pallor, but not quite the same tone as the elderly. Thick hair and smooth skin made them look more sickly than dead. The slack jaw made them appear to be in a deep sleep, or passed out after a night of drinking.

The girl's short hair was a mess. Morty pulled his comb out and arranged it.

Once it was all prepared, he sat down in a chair to wait. He wished Peter would hurry. He enjoyed preparing the body for transport almost as much as embalming, but waiting was boring.

•••

"I don't want a vacation. I love what I do. It's important."

"Look, Morty, you haven't taken a vacation in four years. I could get in trouble from the Department of Labor." As the owner of the mortuary, Mr. Dellinger always worried about the Department of Labor, OSHA, and other agencies. He sat behind his large, dark desk, a grim reaper giving Morty bad news.

"If I don't want to take time off, how can you make me?"

"Morty." He leaned forward, elbows on the desk, and steepled his fingers. "It is not healthy. The job you do is important, but it is difficult. I commend you for being so enthusiastic about a job a most people wouldn't do. But everyone needs a break. It's healthy."

"I don't. Time off is what depresses me."

He sighed. "Surely there are things you like to do. A hobby? Somewhere you'd like to travel? Family to visit?"

Morty shrugged. "Not really."

Mr. Dellinger sat back, looking at him like a suspicious schoolmaster. He waved his hand and stood. "No matter. You have to take a vacation. Two weeks."

"Two weeks?!"

"Yes."

"You are forcing me to take a vacation?"

"I am. Now, please—" He indicated the door.

"Fine." Morty stood.

"Thank you. I will see you in two weeks—"

"I have to leave now?!"

"—I will see you in two weeks. Find something to do. Go somewhere bright and sunny. I promise you will be better for it."

"No, I won't," he said over his shoulder as he walked out of the office.

•••

It had only been three days. Eleven more to go. He was not going to make it.

He tried reading. Watching TV. He took a walk. Fine activities, but so purposeless! Preparing bodies after death is what mattered. Properly and with dignity. He was sure the others did not do it as well.

He knew they didn't understand. They focused on the fact of a dead body, as if there was something morbid about it. That was wrong. Bodies just changed form. Did people possess a soul? Was there was an afterlife? He didn't know and didn't care. The old form transformed into something else, and should be treated with compassion. That's what mattered. What was that so hard for others to understand?

The doorbell rang, and he jumped up. Maybe they'd come to ask him back! They'd realized how much they needed him.

No. They'd call, not come to his door.

It was Mrs. Rose, his neighbor. "Hello, Morty, sorry to bother you. I wonder if I could ask you a big favor."

"Sure." What else did he have to do? Last summer, she asked him to feed their dog while they were at a clinic for a week. Just before Christmas, she asked him to check in on her husband when she was out of town to visit her sister over the weekend. Both were elderly, and Mr. Rose had health problems.

"Well, I hope this isn't another imposition. I have to drive down to Campbell tomorrow morning and have a procedure—I have to stay for three days. Paul doesn't want to go, and he probably shouldn't. I know he'll be fine, but…well, frankly, I'd just feel better if someone checked in on him."

"Happy to, Mrs. Rose. As it happens, I'm off work for a week or so."

"Oh, you are such a dear. Ah—" She blushed. "—don't tell him I asked. Just act like it's your idea."

Morty smiled. "Of course."

"He wouldn't like it if he knew I asked, and he probably doesn't need it. I'm being silly."

"I understand. Happy to do it. Won't say a word."

"And…if you could ask if he took his medicine before lunch and dinner. Here's our extra key in case something happens and he can't get to the door."

She thanked him again and left, still apologizing.

At least he'd have something to distract him.

•••

He had lunch with Mr. Rose that afternoon. They chit-chatted. He'd had heart surgery nine months earlier, and was still dealing with complications of the healing process, including a bout with the flu a month ago. Diabetes exacerbated his problems, along with a urinary tract infection. Morty didn't want all those details, but Mr. Rose felt like sharing.

Morty could see that it tired him to talk so much, though.

"Do you need to take a rest, Mr. Rose?"

"Ah, yes, as a matter of fact. This new medication makes me so tired."

"Did you take your medicine before we ate?"

"Yes, yes, I did. I think I did. Maybe we could check?"

"Of course."

Morty took his arm and led him into the bedroom. Mr. Rose showed him his medicine, arranged in plastic containers with little compartments for morning and evening, for seven days. Tonight's compartment was empty, so he had taken it. Mr. Rose climbed into bed and struggled with the sheet and blanket. Morty helped him.

"Thank you, young man." He closed his eyes and seemed to be asleep in no time.

Morty stood for a moment, watching the slow rise and fall his chest. He wasn't preparing a body, but he was helping him with physical needs. Help for a short sleep rather than the long sleep. He bent down and peered at Mr. Rose's face. It was not gray, but his jaw had slacked. Morty felt an urge to arrange the old man's hair. He reached for his comb, almost out of habit, but withdrew his hand.

After a while, he left the house, locking the door with his key.

•••

Morty and Mr. Rose repeated the routine at dinner. This time, though, Mr. Rose wore his bedclothes. Morty gave him his nightly medication and helped him to bed.

"Thank you, Morty. You are a good neighbor."

Morty smiled and placed his hand on Mr. Rose's head. "Happy to help, Mr. Rose. See you tomorrow."

The next morning, after a brief hesitation, he went next door and knocked.

"Good morning, Mr. Rose. I wonder if you've had breakfast yet?"

Mr. Rose cackled. "Well, yes, but I get up about 4:30, so that was a long time ago. I'm game for a second, if you are."

Morty made eggs and coffee. He stayed until lunch, talking and watching television with Mr. Rose. Better than sitting in his house alone, wishing he was at work.

After he put Mr. Rose to bed that night, he drove to the mortuary. Everyone should be gone except the night clerk. Jimmy didn't do much except phone Mr. Dellinger if a call came in for a pickup.

He used his key to enter. Jimmy sat at the front desk, watching a video on his phone.

"Hey, Mort, what are you doing here? Thought you were on vacation."

No one called him Mort. "I am, but I forgot something. I'm out of town tomorrow, wanted to pick it up."

"Oh, ok. Well, have a good time."

"Thanks."

Morty walked to the back room, glancing back to make sure Jimmy returned to his video.

It did not take him long to collect the items he needed. He put them in a grocery bag from the break room.

"Bye, Jimmy," he called out as he left.

•••

"Paul? I'm home!"

She set her bags down just inside the door. The lights were off. She frowned and turned on the lamp beside the couch. "Paul?" The kitchen lights were off, too. She pushed away an incipient panic. Maybe he'd gone to bed early.

She entered the bedroom and screamed.

TEN MORE DAYS

Ten more days.

They said ten more days.

I shifted in my bed, trying to get comfortable. It didn't work. It never did. I need to get up!

They said ten more days.

The door slapped open with a nurse as the driving force. Without a glance, she went to the clear bags hanging beside my bed. With her left hand, she lifted each one and inspected the contents, traced the tube coming out, then lowered each bag back to vertical. One, two, three, four bags. Same routine for days—or had it been a week—since the surgery. Next, she would examine the machine that each tube entered, with more pipes and wires that exited from the other side and attached to my body. The machine's function was a mystery, though I had asked repeatedly. I prefer to know everything being done to me. I was sure it was something to do with monitoring my various systems and supplying to the proper amount of medications or whatever. Why wouldn't they tell me?

The nurse followed the tubes and wires from the machine to my arm, inspected the insertion points or attachments to my veins or skin. I sometimes fantasized about pulling them all out. One after the other, with a sticky sucking sound and a pop. It would be easy, I guessed. I've seen people do it in movies. Perhaps not an accurate source. Would the needle holes bleed much? Would alarms go off? How long would it take for someone to come rushing in, intent, professional, and in stat mode? "Stat?" Isn't that what they say? I don't know what that means. I'd time the period between yanking them out and when they came in using the second hand on the wall. I couldn't get up—at least not now. Maybe soon. Maybe I could stumble to the chair by the window. I'd be sitting there, casually, when they burst in. That would be amusing.

As she checked one of the needles in my arm, her eyes flicked up to mine.

"Oh, I didn't know you were awake. We gave you a sedative only two hours ago."

"I told them I didn't want it."

"You need to sleep. Help you heal."

"I've slept enough. What does that machine do?" I nodded my head at it, about all I was capable of for now.

"I told you yesterday. In detail. Since you are awake, would you like me to let in any visitors who might come?"

"No. I told them not to come back until I was ready to leave."

She made it clear she disapproved.

She patted me on the arm, contradicting her demeanor, and turned to leave. "Very well. I'll check back later to see if you change your mind. About visitors or sedatives."

As the door swooshed shut, I glanced down at my sheet-covered body. If I am leaving soon, I need a plan. During the time I'd been here, I had given some thought to it. Only ideas for now. I didn't want to keep living in the same boring retirement center. Always eating dinner alone. Watching the grandchildren on Tuesdays while Ellie went to the gym and ran errands. Going to Starbucks and seeing the regulars—both the baristas and customers. Tired of it. Joking with them, pretending to be a happy, retired old man. Needed a change. So I had a lot of ideas. Good ones. But right now, it was all theory. Good places to start, but I should work out the details. Details of how to make a new start.

I had started over before in my life. When I was working. Failed projects. Failed ventures. My first business was an epic disaster. Repercussions lasted over a decade. After the collapse, I told myself that I was "starting from scratch." And it was okay. In fact, I liked it. Reinventing oneself was an exciting adventure.

In comparison, however, I had not been starting from scratch. *This* was starting from scratch. A genuine *tabula rasa*. Like going back to the womb and being born a second time. Except that this newborn has to deal with the loss of a spouse, sickness, loss of a career, and a lot of dead friends. And this stupid surgery as a wrench in the works.

Ten more days. Then I'll get…go…get…. Did that meddling nurse give me sedative without me knowing?

The room was different. Dark. Furnished like an office. Even the bed was different—a large four-poster, with a thick comforter. Nice. But why would they change it around? Maybe they moved me while I was out. The machines were still here, with its attendant tubes and sensors.

A slim figure was sitting in the chair. I had *said* no visitors! I'd seen him before, but I never saw him come in. Or how he got past the nurse's station.

I'd never met him until I came here. I called him the "argumentative interlocutor." Not sure why, other than the fact that he was always arguing with me. And he interlocuted.

"You still have experience and knowledge," he offered.

"Yeah, so? It's all in one career. So does no good when I can't do the same work. That's like telling someone who has the expertise to fly a plane that they are experienced when they can't fly planes anymore."

"It's still not like starting from the womb."

"I'd *prefer* starting from the womb."

"Perhaps," the interlocutor nods, "but your story continues—right to this moment. The next part remains to be written."

"Does it?"

"Maybe. If you survive. I'm not convinced you will. They did a number on your heart. Not all stories end the way you want. Not all novels have a happy ending. Some just fade away."

I told him what he could do with his literary platitudes, and where he could go after he performed the deed.

"Just stating facts."

"Those are opinions. I will walk out of here. They told me ten days."

The figure shrugged. "Maybe."

If I had the strength, I'd have thrown something at him. "You don't think so?"

"Maybe you will. But we don't get to write our own endings."

"Yes, we do."

"No, we don't."

I rolled my eyes. "Then who does?"

He shrugged. "The Fates? The Cosmic Author? The God of the Hebrews? A Pantheistic Director? I just know *we* don't."

"Fine. Agree to disagree. Why are you telling me this?"

"You ought to prepare."

"For?"

"For the end."

"It's not the end."

"It might be."

"It isn't. They said ten days."

Now he rolled his eyes, though I couldn't see his face in the darkness. It felt like he rolled his eyes.

Why did I care what this bastard said? Ten more days and I'd leave this place. Sure, there might be some recovery time at home. But I'd be on my way to a new life.

The door flew open, and another nurse came with a tray. "How are we this morning? Ready for breakfast?"

"It's not morning."

"Oh, but it is! A beautiful one, too."

Why did everyone in this place have to argue with me? She set the tray down on the bed table and opened the drapes. Light poured in. Sunlight.

"How…?" I blinked. They were tricking me. "That's not sunlight. The other nurse was just in here not long ago."

"That was nine hours ago, dear. You slept quite well."

"I didn't sleep at all! I refused the sedative. Are you working with *him*?" I waved, as near as I could, to the man in the chair. But he was no longer there. "Oh. Well, he left."

I despised the sweet look she gave me. "No, dear, we would never try to deceive you. We're here to help you. It's the medication. Makes one a little confused. It will get better. Here's your breakfast."

She removed the lids from the little dishes, the cellophane wrap from the cups, and pushed the table over the bed in front of me. Coffee in a tiny plastic mug. Orange juice in a tiny plastic clear cup. A small container with eggs and toast. No butter. Jam.

"Why is the food here designed for a child? Do leprechauns prepare it?"

She laughed without humor. "If you finish this and want more, I'll get you more."

"No, I don't even want this."

"I know. But you need to eat."

"Why? I'll be out of here in ten days, and I can eat real food."

She paused. "Ten days?"

"That's what you told me."

"I don't—."

"Not you in particular. You people. Someone. A doctor."

"Oh. I didn't know that." She paused again. "Well, you need to eat because that's what people do. They eat breakfast, lunch, and dinner. So eat. Do you need some help?"

Yes, I did. I was too weak not to spill it. "No."

"Okay. I'll come back in a few moments and see how we are doing."

How "we" are doing. Why did she talk in the plural? Was it the royal "we"? Was she the Queen of the Hospital? Was it the editorial "we"? She's the editor-in-chief of medicine? So ridiculous.

No matter. Ten more days and I am out of here.

Crawling. Something crawling all over the wall. Insects. What was wrong with this place? What a dump. It was freaking me out. Where was the button? The control thing.

"Yes?" She was by my side.

"Where's the other nurse?"

"Which one?"

"The one who brought me breakfast."

"Oh, her shift ended."

"What time is it?"

"Ten p.m."

They were screwing with me. But why? Maybe they wanted to keep me. More money for them.

"Can't you do something about the bugs all over the wall? Surely the health inspectors wouldn't take kindly—"

She tilted her head. "Bugs?"

"Yes, bugs. Right *there*." I raised a hand at the wall.

She turned and looked. "There aren't any bugs. I think it's—"

"They are *all over* the wall. How can you not see them?"

"It's your medication. Probably set too high. There are no bugs. Let me see what we can do." She left the room.

"Told you."

He was really irritating me.

"Told me *what*?"

"You know."

"I *don't* know! Half the time you make no sense. Why are you here? I told them I didn't want any visitors."

He shrugged. "Yet here I am."

"What does that mean?"

"Just as I told you before. You don't get to write the story."

"Nurse! *Nurse!*" My hand scrambled for the control.

The door thwacked open. "What do you need, Mr. Dodderson?"

"I said *no visitors*."

"Yes. We know."

"Then why did you let him in?!"

She approached. "One of your medications is a bit high and making you see things. We've lowered the dosage, but it may take a while to wear off. The doctor will visit in the morning, Just ignore the bugs."

"Bugs?" I glanced at the wall. They were gone. No, still a couple. But they were lethargic. Like they were dying.

"Not the bugs. It's *him*." I started to point, but she was gone. How did she leave so fast? I looked at the chair. He was gone, too.

What a terrible place. They should not play tricks on a patient.

Oh well. Ten more days.

"Do you want me to open the orange juice?"

I jerked. "Don't sneak up on me like that."

"Oh, I'm sorry. I thought you heard me come in and open the curtains. The doctor will be here soon."

It was light. What manner of lights were outside that they could make it look like day and then like night so easily? Maybe my room was in a large studio, set up to *look* like outside—sky, city lights, car noises. They can change it whenever they want to play with my mind. It's not right.

"Can you hear me, Mr. Dodderson?"

I remember him. He did the surgery. Doctor…something.

"Hi, Doc. Ten more days and I go home, right?"

He straightened up. "I am not sure. The surgery went well, but you really aren't—"

"You *told* me ten days!"

"I do not recall saying that. When was that?"

"Right before surgery! You said, ten more days."

He shook his head. "If I said that, I misspoke and I apologize. In any case, it's been three weeks since the surgery.

I stared at him, my heart pounding. He was lying. Like all of them. What do they want from me?! My eyes bugged out of my head. I could not speak. Were they doing something to my voice, too?!

"We are doing everything we can to make you comfortable. I think we had your hydromorphone too high, and that caused hallucinations. You should be okay now. But let the nurses know if the pain is too much. We might try oxymorphone.

What was he playing at? "What hallucinations?"

"You saw something crawling on the wall."

"Yes, but they're gone. What about the guy who sits in the chair?"

He had turned away and was whispering to the nurse. Something about me, something devious, I was sure. He turned back. "What was that?"

"Nothing. When can I get out of here?"

He sighed. Was that pity on his pasty face? I hate him. He turned, pulled a chair over beside the bed, and sat down. He fixed me with his medical eyes, his medical mouth pursed in a medical grimace.

"Mr. Dodderson. We have had this conversation. I know you have been through a lot. But I also know you have no memory problems. It is doubtful you will leave here any time soon. Your heart and lungs, they are in bad shape. As you know. The surgery kept you from having a massive heart attack. But you are weak. Recovery takes a long time at your age."

My age. What a bastard.

"I ask you for patience. I promise we are doing everything we can to make you comfortable. To help you heal."

I quit listening. I don't need someone to pander to me.

Besides, ten more days until I can finally get out of here.

"You aren't going anywhere."

It was a slim figure sitting in the chair. I'd seen him before, and I never knew how he got in, or how he got out. Where did the doctor and the nurse go? Probably didn't want me to remind them that I didn't want any visitors.

I remember him. I call him the argumentative interlocutor. He's irritating. I should ask the nurses to deny any visitors. "You need to go. Besides, the doctor said ten more days, and I could leave."

"No, he didn't. More importantly, he said, 'we're trying to make you comfortable.' You know what that means."

"It means they are trying to make me *comfortable*. Until I can leave. *In ten days.*"

"No. When doctors and nurses say that, they have given up. Their job is to heal you. Once you can't be healed, they do their best to make you 'comfortable.'"

"You make no sense."

"Oh, but I do. I make the most sense. I'm the most sensible person you have ever met."

Ten more days. Can't wait to get out of here.

The door thumped open. I heard an alarm. Was it a fire? Am I being evacuated? Maybe this was the day I leave. The alarm is a celebration.

People around me. Being moved, jostled, poked. I can hardly see. Why is it so smoky in here? Run a fan!

"Mr. Dodderson? Can you hear me? I need you to open your mouth."

Breakfast again?

"…not responding…awake…intubate…raise the…"

Something was making me gag. I can't breathe. This food is terrible. Making me sick now.

"Mr. Dodderson, you need to stop trying to talk. Try to relax."

Why were they always bugging me? Oh well, I should relax. Wouldn't be long now. Ten more days.

WHAT DOES THE RIVER SAY?

What does the river say?
It muſt move along.
Sometimes slow, frequently faſt.
Sometimes peaceful, sometimes furious.
Cold or warm, clean or polluted.
Full of life, full of waiting
Even when frozen over,
There is movement below.

What does the river say?
Keep moving
To pause is to perish.
Even blocked, dammed, rerouted:
Move a little.
Nurture life.
Stay fresh.
Alive.
Keep ſtirring.

What does the river say?
It says that it must flow.
Time moves, the universe goes.
Entropy and extropy.
The road to meaning.
Always, ever, and forever.
And so the river flows.
Sometimes creeping, sometimes rushing.
Sometimes smooth, sometimes coarse.
Keep moving.

What does the river say?
My action has purpose.
And order.
Guided by the weather, the terrain;
The earth's revolution, the sun, the stars.
Keep moving.
Movement is value.
Where or how or when
Is sometimes remote.
But keep moving
because I believe it.

•••

I am born in cataclysm. Heat, light, dark, matter, gas. Explosions, coalescence, collisions, revolving, flying. Gravity tugging this way and that way. I am reeling. Spiraling. Dizzy.
   Then silence. Motion slows. Stops.
   Cooling.
   Darkening.

Time.
No time.
Eternity.
Movement. Light and delicate.
Movement. Faster and stronger.
Movement. A calamity in the distance. I am sheltered.
Touchdown. Transport. Silence.
Sound breaks silence. Muffled. Hammer. Chisel.
Louder?
Crack!
Silence, then resumption. Tap. Tap. Tap. A fragment of me is gone. Time and tapping and crack! And silence. A pattern, minor fluctuations, virtually imperceptible .
Sound, silence, hammer, chisel, crack. Chipping away. At me.
The rock, the stone, the capping of basalt. Mining in a ward. Slow and deliberate, the exterior chips aside. Breaks away. Chunks detach, spiraling off in space.
The core is exposed. The compressed matter, born out of the cataclysm. A pure being, an invented being, a product of formation.
Crack! Light! It burns, also there is enjoyment. Sharp pain with the potential of liberation. Open. Free.
Only a slight part, but light reaches it. The air touches it. Like a shell of chillingÂ lava opening to life below. I wait for the tap. The next crack. The growing touch of light and air. Pain. And delight.
Shards. Anticipatory silence. Tentative tapping.
Crack!
Light!
The tiny opening grows. Warmth, light, air—creation opens to me, so gradual as to generate pain—but it

opens to me. I see…I see…time and being and purpose and prospective. Now future. Firm nurture. Fine nature. Finally naked. Freedom.

I stand unveiled in my created state. Air, water vapor, light, surface, skin, bone, fluids and…me. As I was created in the beginning, as I stood without shell, without protection, without mask. I am naked before all of creation.

I am afraid.

•••

Hello?

Silence.

Is someone there?

Movement.

Who…who are you?

A slight tingling in my feet. Little spindly insects, scrabbling and jerking their gossamer legs. Slow spread up shins, knees, thighs. Not creatures. Electrical pulse. Nervous energy. Blood flow. Torso. Outward to arms. Between shoulder blades.

Movement.

Who are you? What are you?

Verm. I am verm.

Verm? What is that? Your name? What you are?

No answer. It was small. Nervous, like a little mouse. A little varmint, nibbling with its tiny teeth and scratching with its tiny claws. So tiny I can only detect it by remaining still and silent. Motionless, fixated on the sensation.

Stomach. A slight *push*, a slight ache, a trace of indi-gestion. But not enough to recognize unless holding quite still.

Why are you here?

To tell you.

To tell me what?

Take care.

Take care of what?

Pause.

Â I waited. Shallow breathing.

Time. The moment.

Frowning. What did that mean?

I waited. Shallow breathing.

A still, insignificant sound of a scratch. Nails on a wall.

I waited.

Are you in pain?

No.

Are you tense?

I suppose. A little. Busy day.

What are you avoiding?

What?

What are you avoiding?

I…I don't know. You, I guess. Or I was.

What about me?

The little teeth. The scratching. Movement.

Why?

Why what?

Why are you ignoring it?

I suppose because other things are more important. Work. Family. Life. Everything a person should do.

They aren't.

What isn't?

They aren't significant. They count. But not important.
I don't agree.
Of course you don't. Do ut des.
What?
You only said "family" because you think you should.
I did not.
Wrong.
Rather talkative suddenly, aren't you Varm—what was your name?
Verm.
Verm. What kind of name is that?
Change the subject.
What?
You changed the subject.

•••

What does the river say?
It says that I must move along.
Sometimes slow, sometimes fast.
Sometimes peaceful, sometimes angry.
Ease or struggle, obstacles or free way
Full of life, full of waiting
Even when diverted
There is movement.

What does the river say?
Keep moving
To pause is to die
Even if you can barely move
Move a little
Make a decision
Stay fresh

Working.

What does the river say?
It says it muſt move along
Be good, ſtruggle ſtrong, moving ahead
Integrity and focus
The way to meaning
It is the way of the universe.
And so I move
Never doubting, knowing truth,
All will be fine, it will work out.

What does the river say?
My movement has purpose
And direċtion
Steered by honeſt intentions, belief in myself,
The good in humans, in myself, in way of life.
Not work for work's sake
Though I regularly do not know
Precisely where or how,
I truſt, I aċt, I believe.

OVER THE BAR

It felt like—finally—they appreciated his knowledge and skill. Some might have wondered if he wasn't jealous of Maria, who had been promoted to manager at the same time. But "lead bartender" was much more satisfying to Theo. It meant control. It meant teaching.

He did hate the daily preps, though. How could getting ready for such ecstasy be such drudgery? Unlocking the cabinets. Pulling out all the bottles and arranging them on the shelves. One hundred and fifty-seven! Why the hotel wouldn't spend the money for locking cabinets was beyond him. Going over to the main office to get the cash. Set up the registers. Make sure the well was stocked and ready. Prepping the garnishes, the mixes, the juices. Checking the freshness of the milk and cream. Logging breakage. Setting out the glasses like neat soldiers, each platoon with its own characteristics: tumbler, Collins, rock, red-wine, white wine, shot, flute, and so on. His past pride in knowing each item's history and function still gurgled below the surface. But it paled in light of what he could do with it all. Satisfying. Titillating. Arousing, even.

As he placed the last bottle of gin on the shelf, he caught a movement out of the corner of his eye. Bobby, leaning against the far end of the bar, looking at his phone.

"Bobby! Fill the ice!"

Bobby nodded, not even bothering to look up. The young guys were worse than the girls who tended or waitressed. At least the girls appeared to have some desire to do a good job, even if they were incompetent. The guys didn't care that they would never get a good recommendation. The job was an imposition on their fun and screen time.

He shook his head. He often considered teaching them a lesson, too. It would be more difficult, though. Employees weren't supposed to drink except to check a complex cocktail with a cocktail straw, or ensure freshness of an ingredient. Bar backs didn't do that, of course. It was much easier to work his magic with a customer. He chuckled to himself at that image. He was a magician or a sorcerer—mixing and doling out potions.

Jessie rushed in from the back, fifteen minutes late. "I'm sorry, Theo, you already did all the bottles! You shouldn't have to do it yourself."

Despite her words, Theo knew it was her plan. She hated climbing up and down the stepladder.

"It's okay. I don't mind." He *did* mind, but mostly as it reflected on her and her generation. He liked her because she respected his skill. She often asked his opinion as they worked, she defended him to coworkers or the manager when necessary. Not that it happened often— Theo was much too careful. He was not going to do anything to endanger this perfect job.

A few guests had already wandered into the lobby area, one had sat down near the end of the bar. Theo recognized him from last night, talking with a few people. Theo listened in surreptitiously using his usual methods. The man mostly complained about his boss, his coworkers, and the current conference in session at the hotel. When Theo asked if he was ready for another drink, he said, "No, one gin and tonic and beer is my limit. I've learned not to overdo it at these stupid conferences. I start to say what I think." He and Theo laughed in a shared understanding. So Theo had printed out his bill, handed it to him, and settled up. He got a nice tip, but more importantly, some information that could be used later in the week, perhaps.

•••

Theo scanned the room. It had filled up. Mostly with the conference attended, but a few others, too. He didn't recognize the three by one of the standup tables, but there were two sitting on the couch who had been here last night. The rest of the room was a mixture of those he recognized, some new ones, and a few he'd been keeping his eye on.

He wandered down to the end of the bar, making a blatant show of checking if anyone's drinks needed attention. When he reached the end, he adjusted some bottles behind the bar, then turned to face the man sitting alone.

"Good evening, sir. How was your day?"

The man looked up from his phone. "Pretty boring. Session after session of stuff I already know. My boss chattering incessantly in my ear. The only good thing was that I had a few moments to sit out by the pool. This is nice place."

"Yes, we are lucky to be able to work here. The pool is nice. Can I get you a gin and tonic?"

"You remembered! Yes, thank you. I've had my beer."

"I usually do remember the more classy customers. Is the house gin still OK?"

"Yes."

"Gin and tonic, coming right up."

He selected a double rocks glass and filled it with ice from the bin below. With the bottle of house gin in one hand and the gun in the other, he held the short-pour button for the tonic to mix about 50% more gin than usual. A lime wedge, wiped around the rim and dropped in, finished it off. He set the glass down on a bar napkin down. "Anything else for now?"

"No that's great. Going to watch the game." He nodded at one of the televisions mounted behind the bar. Theo glanced back. A baseball regular-season game.

A woman and a man were just taking seats near the middle of the long curved bar top. As he approached, he saw they were arguing. Pretending not to notice, he asked if they would like anything.

"I'll have a bourbon, neat, Knob Creek if you've got it," set the man. "She'll have a glass of your white house wine."

"I can order from myself," she said in clipped words. She glanced up at Theo. Pretty eyes, but angry. "I'll have a Cosmopolitan."

"Cosmopolitan?!" the man said. "Since when did you start drinking cocktails?"

"Since tonight." She looked at Theo with triumph.

Theo nodded. "Bourbon and a Cosmo, coming right up."

He watered the bourbon, but not as much as he might have in other circumstances. The guy specified the bourbon; a clue that he had a more refined taste than most. Theo was aware that it could be because he thought it sounded cool, or because he was from Kentucky, or some other reason. But he never took chances. On the other hand, a customer's first Cosmo meant a generous pour of vodka.

●●●

It was crowded now. More so than usual because of the conference. They drink here in the late afternoon, then leave for dinner, then come back for more. Some stay far later than they should, with conference sessions starting at 8am.

He had spotted a woman sitting down at the end of the bar alone. Young. Attractive. Dressed pretty casually—probably not here for the conference. Tina had served her a vodka martini. These kids didn't appreciate the classics.

At the moment, she was staring into her drink, which was almost empty. He glanced around.

"Jessie, is Tina on break?!"

Without looking up from the register, she said, "Yeah about five ago. You going after her?"

"No, I'm fine. You can go next."

He approached the woman.

"Can I get you another?"

She looked up, startled. Her eyes showed Theo that she had been drinking before she arrived. And crying, by the look of her mascara.

"Uh, yeah, why not?"

"Vodka martini?"

"Yeah, with a blue cheese-stuffed olive."

He rolled his eyes as he walked away. Regular olive or a lemon peel slice was not good enough for anyone these days. They probably didn't even know that lemon was an option—too classy and simple.

He made the drink, heavy on the vodka, and served it to her with a napkin underneath while picking up the empty glass. He suspected she was at a moment where he could gain some information.

"Are you okay, miss?"

She held his eyes for a second or two, seeming to have a debate with herself. "Not really. Sucky day."

"Oh, I'm sorry to hear that." It was always best to stay neutral and give just a tap here and there. If the person was a good fit, they'd tell him far more than he would get if he asked.

She took a sip, then leaned forward. Here it comes, Theo thought. "My boyfriend is a jerk. Don't know why I don't break up with him."

"Ah," he said, nodding. "Guys can be awful. Never know how good they have it, then if you leave, they are suddenly so nice, wanting you back."

She slapped the bar top. "*Exactly!* Every time I tell him I have had it with him, he starts being all attentive and sweet. Then, after a few weeks, we're right back where we were. Ignores me, flirts with other girls, tells me how stupid I am."

What an empty-headed girl. "It's a story I hear a lot. So sad."

She looked up with interest. "So what would you do?"

Again, don't give answers. Let them take the line and run with it. He pursed his lips to look thoughtful. "I don't know. Guess it depends on how much you love him."

Empty-Head slumped back. "That's the problem. I love him a lot. When things are good, it's wonderful. We've talked about a wedding date. But he hasn't even proposed!"

"Well, if you are planning on getting married, then maybe it's worth working. through."

"Yeah. But I want him to *propose*. Be romantic. He says it's dumb. He says if we both already know—" Her phone played a melody. Ariane Grande or something. She pulled it out of her purse hanging on the bar chair and looked at the screen.

"Ahh! It's him. I don't wanna talk right now." She tapped the screen and set it down on the bar.

"Relationships can be so difficult," Theo said. "Someone as attractive and as smart as you are shouldn't have to deal with it. But if he's worth it…"

She smiled. "He is. I think he is. He's just a jerk sometimes."

Theo nodded. "Here, let me get you a drink. On the house. What would you like? Something different?"

"Aw, that's nice. Yeah, I wanna do a shot!"

Perfectly predictable.

"Choice? Or would you like me to surprise you?"

Empty-Head smiled. "You pick! Thanks."

He went back to the bar. They had a cask strength whiskey somewhere. It was a special, so he'd have to pay for it. But with his discount, it might be worth it.

•••

He scanned the bar once again. The couple were into a pretty good argument now. The woman was quite drunk and getting a little louder. Perhaps it was time to goose him. The conference people are beginning to arrive after their dinners. Gin-and-Tonic man approached the bar and waved without emotion.

"Another gin and tonic, sir?"

"Make it a double." He leaned toward Theo as he took his seat. "You ever had to work with a real jackass?"

"Oh, yes. Not here of course."

"Well…" he turned and looked over his should. "See that piece of work in the dark green polo? Waving his hands around?"

"I see him."

"At dinner, we're all splitting the bill, and he decides he doesn't want to split it up evenly. I'm telling him it's *easier*. What's a few dollars. Gets written off on expenses anyway. But he insists, because his dinner was *three bucks* cheaper than everyone else's. I'm telling him off, then this bitch who has a crush on him tells to just go ahead and figure it out."

"Some people, huh?"

"Yeah. No big deal for her, she didn't have to figure it out. I'm in no mood to do math!"

Theo shook his head and set down the double gin and tonic. Which was actually a triple. "Here's your drink. On the house."

He nodded. "Thank you. You are a good bartender."

"My pleasure." *You have no idea.* "Excuse me for a moment."

A young man, who had arrived a little while earlier, was drinking a beer that Jessie had served him. Theo noticed he had been focused on his phone the entire time since he sat.

"Evening, Boss, can I get you another beer?"

He looked up at Theo. Blank face. Blank eyes. *This is not a smart man*, thought Theo "I'm not finished with this one." Theo recognized the type immediately. One of the current crop of young idiots who spend so much time on their phones they can't communicate in person.

"Yes, but we have five minutes left in happy hour. I'd happy to go ahead and put one on your tab, if you like. No pressure."

"Oh, yeah. Well in that case, yeah."

"What are you drinking?"

"I dunno. Some kind of IPA."

It's bad enough to be unaware of classic drinks. But when you don't even *care* what kind of beer you drink? Everyone should have a favorite or two—and know *why* it's their choice.

He poured a Harpoon from the tap. No reason to waste any of the better IPAs.

"Here you are, Boss, a fine Harpoon IPA."

Young Idiot didn't even look up from his phone. "Thanks."

"Are you meeting someone?"

That got him to pay attention. "Uh, no. Hoping to, if you know what I mean." He laughed.

"Ah, yes indeed. Well, good luck. I'll keep my eyes open for you."

Perfect. An idea was already forming in Theo's mind.

●●●

As he came back from his break, Gin-and-Tonic man called him over. "I need another. But I'm tired of gin and tonic. Whatcha got for me?"

He was good and soused. "Do you like bourbons? Whiskeys? Vodkas?"

He leaned forward. "I like 'em all. Whatcha got?"

A man appeared beside him. "Jim. Mind if I sit?"

It was Gin-and-Tonic man's colleague from dinner. Green Polo Cheap Guy.

Gin-and-Tonic growled. "Whatever."

The man sat. "Hey, let me buy you a drink." The man had been drinking, but was not as far along as Gin-and-Tonic.

"Naw. I'm good. This good man here—" he waved at Theo "—was about to get me something new. Bourbon?"

"Yes," Theo said. "Would you like me to choose?"

"Please do, my friend."

"Rocks or neat?"

"Neat." He turned, with some effort, to Green Polo Cheap Guy. "Tell ya what. Get one for my cheap friend here, too."

Green Polo Cheap Guy sighed. "Come on, Jim, that's not—"

"I said get him one!"

Theo backed away and went to peruse the bourbon section. He was pretty sure they had a bottle of Blanton's—ah, yes, here it is. He filled two rocks glasses, slightly over a typical pour and set them down.

The two were talking, Green Polo Cheap Guy was trying to apologize or explain about the dinner altercation. Gin-and-Tonic was having none of it, still trying to explain the realities of life to the man.

Theo nodded his head and went over to check on Arguing Couple, who waved ambiguously when he came over. He refilled the man's drink. Glancing down at Empty-Head, he saw that Maria, now on shift, was serving her shots of something. Theo enjoyed it when his coworkers assisted without even knowing what they were doing.

•••

Theo nodded to a middle-aged man who approached the bar and sat. He took a seat next to Young Idiot, who was still intent on his phone.

"Good evening. I would like to know if you can make a Vesper Martini."

"Certainly. Traditional or modern?"

The man cocked his head and smiled. "By traditional, are you referring to Kina Lillet and Gordon's gin? Lillet removed the quinine in the 1980s, and Gordon's is no longer the same proof as when Fleming wrote the novel."

It seemed Theo had met a worthy customer. "Indeed. So it depends on whether you want the original *named* ingredients, or a closer approximation of the drink itself."

"The drink itself, of course."

"I could not agree more, good sir. In that case, I suggest Cocchi Americano in place of the Kina Lillet. However, there is still an export version of Gordon's which is 94.6 proof. Which we have."

He looked surprised. "I was not aware of that. I use Bombay Sapphire for the American market, or Tanqueray No. 10."

"Good choices if you cannot find the Gordon's export. For vodka I suggest Stolichnaya Blue to approximate the 1950s proof."

"A fine choice, and mine as well. I shall have a traditional Vesper martini, prepared as you see fit."

"It will be my pleasure."

Theo concocted the drink in a deep champagne goblet, satisfied to know there were still classy people who understood history and mixology. He added a thin slice of lemon peel as the final classic ingredient.

●●●

"May I get you another beer?"

"Ah, no, I think I want a Jagermeister shot," Young Idiot said. "No luck in this place or on Tinder." He was striking out.

"Well, I may have a lead for you. See that young woman down there—the blonde?"

He looked. "At the end of the bar?"

"Yes."

"Nice."

"I have been speaking to her, and she says she is quite lonely and was hoping to meet someone. But she doesn't want to be set up. If you don't mind some advice, just go down and sit by her as if you have just arrived. Don't talk at first, just wait for an opportunity. Take it slow, don't be too forward. I am pretty sure it will work out." Theo was not at all sure Young idiot could follow the instructions.

He smiled. "Well, thank you. You're the boss." He picked up his almost-empty beer glass.

"Let me take that, and I will bring you another. You just got here, remember?"

He nodded. "Oh, yes, right."

Theo poured another beer and took it to him at his new seat, then turned to Empty Head.

"Another shot, miss?"

She looked up through heavy lids. "Sure…yeah…why not?"

"What were you drinking?"

"I…uh…tequila? I don't remember." She giggled.

"Well, may I suggest a Jagermeister. I just served one to this man here, and he loved it."

She looked over at Young Idiot. He raised his glass to her. "Sure, bring me that."

He smiled as he walked away.

He walked down the bar. Arguing Couple were getting louder. Gin-and-Tonic and Cheap Green Polo were engaged in an animated discussion. As Theo walked by, he swept up stray napkins and straws, swiping the Cheap Green Polo's wallet which was still sitting beside him on the bar.

He went around and outside the bar, making a show of straightening empty chairs and checking on customers. He approached Gin-and-Tonic.

"How are you doing, sir? "Theo clapped him on the back, then slid his hand down and placed the wallet in the pocket of his jacket. "Can I get you anything else?"

"Naw, naw, we're good. Just teaching this one how the world works."

"Naw, I think I'm teaching you not to be such a hard-ass." The man stood up. "Where are the bathrooms?"

Theo pointed and returnd to the bar.

●●●

"You *bastard!*"

Everyone in the bar looked at Arguing Couple. Theo allowed himself a small smile. The room fell silent, and, as everyone realized it had become *too* quiet, they started talking again. Some continued to watch the fracas—a few directly, others with sideways glances. Meanwhile, the woman had quieted and sat back down, but was still talking to the man in a low but firm voice. Theo loved these moments when the entire room became a living organism, reacting and moving in shock, anger, and pain.

He approached the couple at a slow pace, making sure they would see him before he got too close. The man was hissing angry words at her, and when he saw Theo, he stopped and looked down at his glass.

"Everything okay here?"

The woman looked at the man and then at Theo. "Yes, thank you. Except that my husband is an ass."

The man shook his head at Theo. "I'm sorry for her. She gets emotional when she drinks. It won't happen again." His eyes brandished daggers, "Right, honey?"

The look she gave him should have melted his face. It was wonderful. She stood up and started to speak, thought better of it, and stormed out.

The man looked at Theo and shrugged a gesture of masculine understanding. "She'll be back and we'll leave. Sorry for the trouble."

"No problem, sir. Would you like anything?"

"Yeah, gimme a beer. Stella."

•••

Theo had been observing Young Idiot and Empty-Head. She was obviously enjoying the attention, though she probably wouldn't remember it tomorrow. She didn't seem to be flirting, though he was trying. That didn't matter. He had been watching closely. Her phone was still on the far edge of the bar where she had set it down earlier. They were so engaged and drunk, now was his chance.

He brought them new drinks and set them down. "On the house." They thanked him without interrupting their gaze upon each other. She was telling him about her boyfriend as he listened with feigned sympathy. As Theo cleared the empty glasses and napkins, he gathered in her phone.

"Going to the john, be right back," he said to Jessie. As soon as he was out of sight, he opened the phone. It was passcode locked, but a screen notification read "Missed call from 'babe.'" He tapped the notification and message opened without unlocking the phone, with two options displayed: "Listen to message" and "Call back." He tapped the latter.

"Babe, what the *hell!* Where are—"

"Sir, apologies, this is a bartender at the Parcourir La Terre Hotel Bar. Everything is fine with your girlfriend, but she is very drunk, and we'd like you to come get her."

"What? Why do you have her phone?"

"As I said, sir, she is very drunk and asked one of our staff to call for her."

"Thanks, man, I'll be right there."

Theo was able to return the phone without her noticing.

•••

"It was right *here*! I left it *here*."

"I didn't take it!"

Exquisite, Theo thought.

"Did you leave when I went to the bathroom?"

"No."

"Then you either took it or saw someone take it."

"Nope. You're so drunk it's probably still in your pocket."

Cheap Green Polo stood up. "You're drunk *and* a bastard. Look—" he stuck his hands in the four pockets of his pants, pulling each one inside out, turning to display the lack of contents. "See?! My keys *and that's it.* You took it!"

Maria, standing at the far end of the bar, began to approach as the argument grew louder. Theo hoped she would not get there too soon.

Gin-and-Tonic stood in turn and pulled out the pockets of his pants, showing them empty except for keys and a container of mints. Then he stuck his hands into his jacket pockets and froze. "What…?" He pulled out the wallet.

"I *knew* it! You lying thief! Thought I didn't pay enough at the restaurant so you—"

"—no I didn't I don't know how—"

By this time Tina had arrived. "Please, please, gentleman—"

"He stole my wallet—"

"—no I didn't—"

"—Please!" hissed Maria. "I will have you both thrown out if you can't settle this quietly."

"I want to call the police. Call the police."

"I didn't do anything!"

Maria placed a hand on each of their arms. "I'm calling security, and they can deal with you. But *please* be quiet." Theo continued to watch the two men as they tried to be quiet. He was pretty sure they did not have the ability.

•••

"You piece of shit! Get away from my girlfriend!"

Theo watched in satisfaction as Young Idiot jumped up from his seat. "What the hell, man! I was just talking to her."

"I'll *bet*!" The outraged boyfriend turned to Empty-Head, who was watching the interaction with eyes that could not focus. She reached out to grab his arm and nearly fell off the stool. "Baby, wait—"

"Shut up, bitch, what the hell are you doing with this piece of shit?!"

"Hey, hey!" Young Idiot said. "You're the piece of shit. We're just having a drink."

Theo saw Maria hurrying over. He hoped she might trip.

"Not with some other guy's girl you don't!" He took a swing and Boyfriend moved too late The punch caught him in the neck, and he stumbled to the site.

Maria was waving at Theo. "Call the police!" She reached them men and put a hand out to each. "Please, please, gentleman. Not in here. The police are on their way."

"Yeah?! I'll gladly take it outside. And you go home, you *whore!*"

"You're crazy," said Young Idiot as Empty Head screamed, "I'm not a whore!"

Theo watched with delight as he dialed the phone.

"Officer Rodriquez."

"This is Theo at the Parcourir La Terre Hotel Bar."

"Hello, Theo. Another fight?"

"Yes. Two guys over a girl."

"Okay, I have a patrol nearby. Dispatching now."

Hanging up, he watched the foursome move and gesture and threaten. Maria had restored some calm. Everyone in the bar was watching. Those nearby had grabbed their drinks and backed away. At the other end, the security guard was listening to Gin-and-Tonic and Cheap Green Polo speak at the same time. Meanwhile, The woman role in Arguing Partner had returned, said a few choice words and stormed out again with her husband trailing behind.

It was a lovely dance, chaotic yet predictable, with small and large patterns. A thing of artistic beauty come to fruition.

Boyfriend grabbed the woman's arm and said something Theo didn't hear. He pulled her up out of the chair, her legs gave out, and she fell, wailing.

"Hey, hey!" Young Idiot said. "Come on!"

"You shut up, shithead, I'll beat the shit out of you." An obviously limited vocabulary, rivaling Young Idiot.

Maria jumped between them again. The woman remained on the floor, crying. To Theo's left, the security guard was pushing Gin-and-Tonic and Cheap Green Polo apart.

The police officers arrived, one each to the two altercations. Maria knelt down to help Empty Head, a hand on the shoulder of the sobbing woman.

Many of the customers had left, which usually happened when things got physical. Understandable, but purely verbal arguments became boring after a while.

•••

"Quite a spectacle," Vesper Man said, after things had calmed down and all parties removed.

Theo nodded. "Yes, it gets that way sometimes. I prefer a more refined crowd, such as yourself, but people come in here to blow off steam sometimes. It's part of the business."

The man nodded. "Add alcohol to the mix, and I can imagine you have seen some crazy stuff."

Theo smiled. "Oh, I could write a book."

The man nodded. "Excellent Vesper, by the way."

"Thank you. Another? It's on the house."

"I'd have said yes even if I had to pay for it. I appreciate an expert mixologist like yourself."

"Thank you. And I appreciate customers like you who know the skill and knowledge required."

The man laughed. "You must want to teach some of these people lesson or two, I guess."

Theo laughed along. "You have no idea."

If you enjoyed this book, please consider leaving an online review. The author would appreciate reading your thoughts, and most sales are prompted by reviews from readers like you.

About the Author

Markus McDowell is an author & editor of fiction and nonfiction. He has a Ph.D. from Fuller Theological Seminary and a law degree from the University of London, and has lectured at universities in the United States, Europe, and the United Kingdom. He is the author of the literary novel, *To and Fro Upon the Earth: A Novel*, an historical fiction novel, *Onesimus: A Novel of Christianity in the Roman Empire*, and nonfiction such as *Prayers of Jewish Women: Studies of Patterns of Prayer in the Second Temple Period*, *Prayer in the Ancient Stoic Tradition*, and a number of books on legal education.

Visit his website at
https://markusmcdowell.com

Subscribe to his newsletter at
https://markusmcdowell.com/newsletter-2/

You can also follow him on social media
Instagram: https://www.instagram.com/_doctor_markus_
Twitter: https://twitter.com/markusmcdowell
FaceBook: https://www.facebook.com/MarkusMcDowellAuthor/

About the Publisher

Sulis International Press published fine fiction and non-fiction in a variety of genres. For more, visit the website at
https://sulisinternational.com

Subscribe to the newsletter at
https://sulisinternational.com/subscribe/

Follow on social media
https://www.facebook.com/SulisInternational
https://twitter.com/Sulis_Intl
https://www.pinterest.com/Sulis_Intl/
https://www.instagram.com/sulis_international/